SEASON OF CHANGE

Other books by Lisa Williams Kline

Sisters in All Seasons Series

Summer of the Wolves

Wild Horse Spring

Blue Autumn Cruise

Winter's Tide

SISTERS IN ALL SEASONS

BOOK FIVE

SEASON OF CHANGE

BY LISA WILLIAMS KLINE

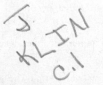

J. KLIN C.1

ZONDERVAN.com/
AUTHORTRACKER
follow your favorite authors

We want to hear from you. Please send your comments about this book to us in care of zreview@zondervan.com. Thank you.

ZONDERKIDZ

Season of Change
Copyright © 2013 by Lisa Williams Kline

This title is also available as a Zondervan ebook.

Visit www.zondervan.com/ebooks

Requests for information should be addressed to:
Zonderkidz, 5300 *Patterson Ave SE, Grand Rapids, Michigan 49530*

ISBN 978-0-310-74007-0

Editor: Kim Childress
Cover design: Thinkpen Design
Cover photography: Mark Jackson
Interior design: Sarah Molegraaf

Printed in the United States of America

13 14 15 16 17 18 /DCI/ 21 20 19 18 17 16 15 14 13 12 11 10 9 8 7 6 5 4 3 2 1

For my parents, Mom and Big D

1

DIANA

I leaned up against Commanche's warm, solid shoulder, rubbing my palms over his leg. His foot was soaking in a bucket of warm water with Epsom salts. He kept kicking at the bucket, trying to pull his foot out. He nickered with annoyance.

"Keep his foot in there!" Josie yelled from another stall. "Twenty minutes!"

I leaned my weight more heavily against Commanche's leg, talking to him soothingly. "It's okay, old boy. Not too much longer." Commanche had gone lame, and the farrier had come today. He'd taken off Commanche's shoe, and drained an abscess. Now we had to soak his foot every day for ten days. And no riding him.

Commanche tossed his head and blew air through his nose. Kicked over the bucket, knocking me right on my butt in the wet straw.

That night, while we were brushing our teeth, I was trying to tell Stephanie about it. "So, anyway, I can't ride him for ten days, and ... "

"Shhh, listen!" Stephanie said. She put down her hairbrush, and touched my arm. I stopped brushing my teeth. We stared at each other in the bathroom mirror, both in our pj's, listening.

When Mom and Norm want to talk about something in private, they go in their bathroom and shut the door. What they don't know is that we can hear every word straight through the pipes that lead up to our bathroom.

"I can't take off work." Norm's voice, louder than usual, came through.

"It's on the weekend. You only have to take one day, Friday." Mom's voice sounded pinched and tight. Like when she was disappointed in me.

"I don't see why we need marriage counseling."

Stephanie gave me a shocked look.

"I just think we have a lot on our plates, like learning to parent each other's daughters. I know I could use some help. And I think you could too."

"Are you still mad I didn't go to Florida to watch Stephanie's cheerleading competition?" Norm asked.

After a minute, Mom answered. "I think one of her parents should have been there to cheer her on.'"

"You were there!" Norm said loudly.

Stephanie blinked and looked away from my face in the mirror.

"Were you mad about that?" I whispered.

She shrugged, not meeting my eyes. "I was fine. I love Lynn."

"I don't understand anything about cheerleading," Norm complained.

"You should learn." I was surprised how harsh Mom's voice sounded.

"I can't believe you're still giving me such a hard time about this!"

"I'm still mad about it!" Mom's voice reverberated through the pipes. "She's chosen to live with us rather than with her mother, which was a really tough decision. And I needed you with me when I had to deal with her father. You know how Diana is, and then add Steven to the mix. I needed you and you weren't there for me."

"I'm there for you!" Norm bellowed.

Stephanie looked at me again. "I don't want to listen to this anymore." She turned and left the bathroom.

Neither did I. "You know how Diana is?" What's that supposed to mean? I know that Mom gets nervous when I'm with Dad. He takes me to do fun stuff that Mom thinks is dangerous, like parasailing. And yes, sometimes he forgets things, like I have to eat. And yes, sometimes he has a few beers and then drives, or loses his temper and yells.

Me going with him over spring break probably gave Mom hives from freaking out, but it had worked because Stephanie had a cheerleading competition in Orlando at the same time. So Mom, Stephanie and I went to Florida for a week but Norm stayed home.

Maybe Norm couldn't go because of work. Or maybe he didn't want to watch some cheerleading competition. I didn't want to go, either, but Stephanie's squad ended up performing right in Disneyworld on the Indiana Jones stage. It had turned out to be pretty cool. Plus, I'd been looking forward to seeing Dad, and things went really well with him for a change. I had alone time with Mom, so I was glad Norm hadn't gone. I didn't want to think about any of it anymore. I finished brushing my teeth, letting my thoughts float back to Commanche.

I headed down the hall toward my room, passing Stephanie's. Above her bed hung a bulletin board plastered with pictures of her friends in their cheerleading uniforms. "Anyway," I said, leaning against her doorjamb, "I can't believe it's summer and I finally have more time to ride Commanche and now I can't ride him!"

Stephanie didn't answer. Then I noticed she was curled on her bed, facing away from the doorway.

"What's wrong?" I asked.

She sat up and wiped her cheeks with the back of her hand, staring at me with a shocked look on her face. "Didn't you just hear the same fight I heard? Aren't you upset? What if they get a divorce, Diana?"

"I didn't think it was that bad," I said, sitting down at the foot of her bed. "Mom and Dad's were way worse."

She rubbed her fingers over her eyes. "Mama and Daddy used to fight a lot and then when they stopped, they just gave each other the silent treatment and I hated that even more."

"Mom and my dad fought twenty-four seven," I said. "At night I used to put my pillow over my head. So, what's the big deal?"

"I just guess I was dreaming," Stephanie said, "thinking that everything between Lynn and Daddy was going to be perfect forever. Nothing is perfect. But when I think about the wedding two years ago, and being the junior bridesmaids, everything seemed so great. And with all the things that have happened, they've always seemed to be really in love." Stephanie pulled her hair back, as if starting to put it into a ponytail, then let it fall back down on her shoulders again. Her hair always looked good. "Do you think they've fallen out of love?" Her eyes looked really scared.

"No!" My heart beat hard a few times. "You're way overreacting, Steph. Relax."

I hadn't wanted Mom to marry Norm. I'd talked back to him, shouted at him, disobeyed him, and treated him as mean as I could. I'd been mean to Stephanie too. And now, well, maybe it would go back to being just me and Mom again. So what? Wasn't that exactly what I'd wanted?

2

STEPHANIE

I couldn't sleep that night. Daddy and Lynn fighting made me feel sick to my stomach. It brought back all kinds of bad memories.

A bunch of people I knew had gone to the beach to celebrate the beginning of summer, so for a while, I texted them back and forth. My phone lit up the darkness of my room.

I got up, went into the bonus room and turned the DVR on low. I watched some TV and painted my toenails the brightest pink I could find.

I couldn't believe Daddy and Lynn were fighting! After Diana and I had been through so much to try to understand each other and get along.

I mean, I'd been counting the days till this summer. I started my first summer job, teaching tumbling and gymnastics to little kids at the Gym Zone. The kids seemed so sweet. I loved it.

Diana just got her license, so she was supposed to help drive me to work. Her driving practically gave me a heart attack, but it was so cool to have our own transportation and our own jobs. She had a job, too — at a fast food place called Cosmic Burgers, where she had to skate out to the cars balancing their orders on a tray.

I hoped Diana and I would keep getting along this summer. I still felt guilty about what had happened to Diana; I'd told my friend Colleen she liked animals better than people and then everyone started calling her "annn-i-mal." Diana said she understood I didn't do it on purpose and she forgave me. She'd even helped me try to get along with my stepbrother Matt.

Now, what if Daddy and Lynn got a divorce? Would I go back and live with Mama? With Matt there? My stomach twisted into a knot. Maybe I'd just go live with Grammy or something.

Just thinking about it made me mess up the polish, and I had to start over. After three coats of polish, I went back to bed.

The next day, I had the worst headache, so I went into Daddy and Lynn's bathroom looking for an ibuprofen. On the counter beside Lynn's makeup case I found a brochure with the title, "Renew Your Marriage." On the front was a picture of a couple standing on a mountain path, with their arms around each other, gazing across the valley to the pale purple mountains beyond. I felt like I was snooping, but I still paged through the brochure, looking at photos of other couples sitting with the counselors. The brochure said that the counselors, Jon and Olivia, were married to each other. Olivia had a kind face and dark wavy hair. Jon had a beard turning gray. On the back of the brochure was a photo of a couple sitting across from each other at an outside cafe, staring lovingly into each other's eyes.

In the middle of one of the pages, I read:

"And if you do decide to divorce, Jon and Olivia can help you navigate this difficult passage. They can help you with breaking the news to the children, with making plans to separate, and with keeping lines of communication open."

A tingle of alarm crept down my neck and shoulders. I put the brochure back where I found it, then headed upstairs and into Diana's bedroom. She was lying on a large stuffed horse she used as a pillow and texting. Probably Noah, that guy from her Spanish class last year. She was always talking to Noah these days.

I stood in the doorway, nervously drumming my fingers on the doorjamb. "There's a marriage counseling brochure in Lynn and Daddy's bathroom."

Diana shrugged. "So?"

"So, it's serious. It's this kind of counseling retreat. These therapists who are married to each other, Jon and Olivia."

Diana sat up and crossed her legs Indian-style, and said, in a theater voice, "*Jon* and *Olivia.*"

"It really scares me."

"Listen, when you compare Mom and Norm's arguments to what used to happen at my house before, they're nothing. Trust me."

"What do you think we should do?" My chin trembled, and I tried to stop it. I hated crying in front of Diana. She was so tough.

"Nothing. Don't tell them that you saw it.

I nodded and wiped my eyes. "Okay. Let's wait and see if they say anything to us."

So when Lynn and Daddy sat us down at the kitchen table a few days later and said they had something to talk to us about, we both acted surprised. I sat in my seat, the one that faces away from the kitchen counter, and glanced over at Diana next to me as she sat in

16

hers, her long blonde hair still flattened from wearing her riding helmet that day. It's funny how we all keep our same seat at the kitchen table. Like each person has their own place in the family. How would it change, if we were all separated?

Lynn traced the outside edge of her placemat, kind of nervous. "Norm and I are going away for a long weekend together."

"Where're you going?" Diana asked.

"To a place in the mountains." Daddy grabbed one of the candlesticks and started using his fingernail to peel away caked candlewax. "Not too far from the ranch we went to a few summers ago."

"But it'll be just us," Lynn added.

"Why would you want to get rid of us?" I said, trying to make it sound like a joke even though my entire insides were shaking. "I mean, we're so perfect and awesome in every way."

"We just need some time to ourselves." Daddy used the tips of his fingers to sweep together a small pile of candle shavings.

"Ooh, TMI, too much information!" Diana said quickly, putting her hands over her eyes.

I laughed, but then I said, trying to sound casual, "So, just a little vacation?"

Daddy cast a look at me, then at Lynn. "Yeah, just

a little vacation," he said, concentrating on the candle shavings.

Diana shot a quick glance at me. "Where will we stay?"

"With Grandma and Grandpa Roberts," Lynn said. "They've been wanting you to come for a visit to the lake, for a while."

Grandma and Grandpa Roberts were Lynn's parents. They lived at Lake Norman, thirty miles north of Charlotte. I'd only met them a couple of times. Usually, when Diana visited them, I was with Mama. "Me, too?" I asked.

"Your mom and Barry had already planned a weekend trip to Asheville," Daddy said. "But Grandma and Grandpa Roberts said they'd love to have you both."

"Wouldn't it seem weird for me to stay with them, since I hardly know them? Maybe I could go to Asheville with Mama," I said, knowing the minute I said it that Mama, and definitely Barry, wouldn't want me coming along. A flush of anger sneaked up my neck. Mama kept asking me to move back, but she was never around when I needed her! Where else could I stay? Maybe with Colleen.

"We thought it would be better if you stayed together," Daddy said. "Since Diana's grandparents offered."

"But what about the Gym Zone? I'm supposed to work Saturday morning."

"Grandpa said he'd take you."

Great. So that argument wouldn't work.

"And I have to go to the barn on Saturday," Diana said.

"Grandpa and Grandma said they'd work it all out."

Diana and I exchanged another look. A long weekend with no friends and no way to get anywhere. With Diana. "I just feel like . . . you're treating us like babies. Why can't we stay on our own? Or why can't I stay with Colleen?"

"I said, because we think it's better if you're together," Daddy said, with a final tone in his voice.

"So . . . what are you guys going to do on your long weekend?" Diana asked.

"Just spend some time together," Lynn said. "Things have been so hectic lately, Norm and I feel like we need to reconnect."

Note to self: They definitely didn't want us to know it was marriage counseling.

"Cool," Diana said noncommittally.

"Great," I said. Which was exactly the opposite of what I really thought.

Later Lynn asked Diana to sweep the back deck and I had to shuck corn for dinner. I sat at the picnic table, tearing off the green husks and the corn silk while Diana swept.

"Mama keeps saying she wants me to live with her, but every time I need to stay with her she's out of town," I said. "I mean, she said she would chaperone the cheerleading trip but that fell through. And now this weekend she and Barry are going on a trip to Asheville." I ripped half a corn husk from an ear. "I'm so mad at her."

"I know how you feel. My dad's done stuff like that lots of times."

"It feels weird to be staying with Grandma and Grandpa Roberts. I've only met them a few times," I said.

"When Mom and Dad were married, we hardly saw them at all, but Mom and I started seeing them more after the divorce. My secret theory is that they didn't like my dad. But they like Norm."

"What's it going to be like, staying there?"

"They're really smart," Diana said. "Both of them were college professors and so they're really into school. And if Grandpa Roberts finds out you can't ski or kneeboard, plan on being out there in the water until you turn into a prune."

"What if I don't want to learn?" My chest tightened with fear.

"Too bad."

I sighed. "Great." I gathered the corn husks and put them in a plastic bag. "Well, I'm going to talk to Mama about this when I have dinner with her this week. Maybe she'll change her mind."

Wednesday when Mama took me to the Italian restaurant near her neighborhood; she started talking about Matt as soon as we sat down. Matt had been drinking last Christmas Eve, wrecked his car, and ended up in the hospital.

"Matt's changed so much since the accident, sugar," she said, after we ordered, as she carefully folded her napkin in her lap, and brushed her hair behind her shoulder. "I believe when he thought he wasn't going to get the movement back in his hand, it really scared him. He was so grateful when it did come back. And now he's got a job at the carwash. And he'll be taking classes at the community college this summer to catch up."

"That's good." But what was I supposed to say? Matt had been nicer to me since the accident. But I knew where this was going.

Mama reached across the red-checkered tablecloth and took my hand. "I want you to move back in with us, sugar. I miss you so much."

I was silent as the black-shirted waiter came and refilled my Diet Coke.

As soon as he left, I pulled my hand away. "I miss you too, but Mama, I really need to stay with you this weekend, and you and Barry are going to Asheville! When I need to stay with you, you're never home!"

"That's just this weekend," she said. "It was just bad scheduling."

"But you missed my cheerleading competition, too! You said you'd chaperone and then you didn't."

"Well, these are both trips Barry and I had planned for a while," she said. "Your father and I never focused on each other the way we should have, to nurture our relationship, and I'm not going to let that happen again."

And then I said the thing I thought I'd never say out loud to her, or to anyone, really. I couldn't help it. It just slipped out. "I just feel like when you have a choice between me and Barry, you always pick Barry."

"Stephanie!" Mama's jaw dropped and her brown eyes went wide. "I can't believe you would think that!"

My face got hot, and I looked away from her. I almost said I was sorry, because I never want anyone to be upset with me. But what I said was true, and then I thought about the way Diana doesn't back down. I set my jaw and glared at Mama.

The server came. "May I take your plates?"

I had hardly eaten any of my ravioli and Mama had barely touched her chicken piccata. We had him box them up and then we didn't speak the whole way home. I was so mad I could cry. When I got out of the car, she didn't say anything. She just looked straight ahead.

"Thanks for dinner," I said in a flat voice. Then I slammed the car door.

Mama had texted me several times since then, but I ignored her.

3

DIANA

A few days after our "family talk" about Mom and Norm's weekend, I called Noah.

"¡Caramba! Se me olvido mi cuaderno," he said. (Which means, "Shoot! I forgot my book!")

"¿De veras? ¡Que lastima! Usted puede pedir prestado de minas," I answered, laughing. (Which means, "Really? What a shame! You can borrow mine.")

This was the way we always opened our phone conversations. He'd been in my Spanish class last semester, and the first time he called me, we'd practiced a Spanish dialogue.

"What are you doing?" he asked now.

"I think my parents are going to marriage counseling." I straightened the horse statues lined on the bookshelf beside my desk. They were kind of babyish, I guess, but I still liked them. Then I lay on my bed, making a pillow from a big stuffed horse Mom had given me years ago for my birthday. "They didn't tell us, but we've figured it out."

"My parents went to marriage counseling. Before they got a divorce," he said.

"That went well." I laughed loudly, pretending it was funny. The reason Noah had moved here in the middle of the year was because his mom had married Kevin's dad.

Then there was a silence between us.

"Noah?"

"Yeah?"

"I don't want to talk about this anymore."

"Me neither."

Last semester, when people were calling me names, and Noah was new, he was the one who asked me why I didn't just punch somebody. After I got back to school from being suspended, I went up to Noah in the hall and yelled at him.

"It's your fault I got suspended!"

"Excuse me?" he said, ducking away from me, pushing his longish, wavy blond hair behind his ear.

"You made me throw my book at her!" I followed him down the hall.

"How did I make you?" He stopped and turned to face me.

"You know what I mean! You're the one who told me to punch somebody."

"I say a lot of stuff," he said. "You shouldn't pay attention to me." We were standing still and people flowed around us like fish in a river. "No one else does."

"I did. I paid attention to you," I said. He was looking at me funny, with these intense greenish-blue eyes.

Two nights later he called me to practice our Spanish dialogue for class, and gradually, we started talking a couple of times a week. And he always said the same thing when I picked up the phone. "Caramba! Se me olvido mi cuaderno." And then one Friday night at a basketball game, when we all went to watch Stephanie's squad perform during half-time, he showed up by himself. Came over and sat next to me on the bleachers. He alternated between two flannel shirts, one mostly green, the other mostly red. His mom was a nurse and worked the night shift, so a lot of times he was on his own for dinner, and Mom started inviting him over. He was teaching himself to play guitar, and he'd bring it and play songs for us. I remember the first song he played for us was "Hey Jude," by the Beatles.

He wasn't my boyfriend. We just hung out. It was cool to have a guy friend. It was cool to have a friend, period.

The next day, work was crazy. By the end of my shift, I was so sweaty from skating into that hot kitchen that my shirt was sticking to me, and the skates were killing my feet. Right before I was about to get off, I brought a burger to some guy with big teeth and he opened it and said, "It's not cooked enough. Take it back!"

I took it back. Brought it back out. He ripped it open, and, without looking at me, said, "Still not done enough." He threw it back onto my tray.

I almost said, "What do you want me to do, buddy, light it on fire?" But I heard Dr. Shrink's voice in my head telling me to count to ten. "I'll get the manager," I said, and skated away from him before I exploded.

By the time Mom picked me up, I was ready to throw something. As I opened the back door to drop my skates on the floor, Mom said "I can't help it, Norm!" into her phone, and then tossed it into the cup holder. Her mouth was set in an angry line. She moved to the passenger seat so I could drive home. "Whew," she said. "You smell like greasy French fries."

"I love you, too." I climbed into the driver's seat, and put on my seat belt. "Oh, my feet are killing me! And why are people so rude to servers? They don't even treat us like humans." I backed out of the parking space and pulled into the lane leading out of the lot.

Normally Mom would commiserate with me, but today she didn't answer. "Look left and check traffic before you pull out," was all she said.

"I know, Mom. You don't have to tell me. I got it!" I said, glancing left..

"I do have to tell you! You haven't got it!" Mom's voice rose. "Or else you already would have done it!"

"Okay, okay! What's with you these days, anyway?" She glanced at me with a guilty look on her face and swept her short blonde hair behind her ear. "Oh, nothing."

"Then why do you and Norm keep fighting?"

"We're not fighting."

"So the yelling and the hanging up the phone are just my imagination."

Mom sighed. "Diana, Norm and I are trying to balance everything and sometimes ... sometimes there's not enough of us to go around, that's all."

I almost told her that I knew about the counseling weekend. It was on the tip of my tongue. But I didn't.

Instead, I said, in a voice imitating Dr. Shrink, "Just remember, Stephanie and I are vulnerable to insecurities about our home and family because of the divorces."

Mom laughed. "Maybe we've had you in therapy too long, Diana."

"It wasn't *my* idea." Though I didn't like therapy at first, now I kind of enjoyed spilling my guts to Dr. Shrink. Who else would sit and listen for fifty minutes while I talked about myself? I'd learned the whole counting to ten thing like I did tonight with the guy with the big teeth. She'd taught me how to rate my moods. I called it the Moronic Mood-o-meter, but it worked. She'd taught me to think about stuff that relaxed me, like being at the barn.

"Don't forget to put on your left turn signal," Mom said. "So many drivers these days don't put on their signals."

"I've got it!" I flipped on the signal.

"Diana, I'm not going to let you drive if you keep acting like this!"

"Okay, okay!"

Sometimes life felt like one big argument.

4

STEPHANIE

Diana and I peered out the windows from the back seat as Lynn turned onto a winding road. It sloped gradually downhill as it meandered toward the water, with these really big oaks and pines shading it from either side. Some of the houses along the shoreline looked old, from the seventies, while others looked new. Little tiny trailers stood next to big two story houses with peaked roofs and circular driveways. In each back yard, graying wooden docks with boatslips stretched into the water. Aluminum pontoon boats floated in some of the boat slips, while cigar boats, ski boats, and sailboats were in others.

"Lake Norman is a huge manmade lake," Lynn told us. "It was made when Duke Power dammed up the Catawba River about fifty years ago. Underneath the water are houses and farms and roads that the rising water swallowed up."

"Weird," I said. "Imagine riding along in a boat and looking down and seeing a chimney or a roof. Or think about the rooms in the houses, with fish swimming through."

"Freaky," Diana said. "And maybe some skeleton with algae sitting in a rocking chair on the porch."

"Don't say that!" I said. Diana was always trying to creep me out. It didn't take much. "Now I won't go swimming!"

"Stephanie being afraid to do something . . . " Diana said. "That would be different."

"Anyway, it took a long time for the water to rise to its peak," Lynn said.

"And then they named it after me," said Daddy with a laugh.

Lynn didn't laugh at Daddy's joke. Was she mad at something Daddy said? Was I reading too much into it?

I'd been watching them every minute to see if they were fighting. I'd started praying at night that they wouldn't get a divorce. I wondered if God was tired of me always asking for things. But I couldn't help it.

I didn't talk to Diana about it because she'd just make fun of me for even praying. For thinking God might find time to listen to my prayers.

Next to me in the back seat, Diana looked out the window into the woods, and I got a text from Colleen.

Guess who's having a party Saturday night?

Who?

Hunter Wendell.

My heart tripped. Hunter had been in my biology class, and I had had a secret crush on him all last semester. He was a swimmer, with big shoulders and small hips. Very quiet and cute. But not even Colleen knew about my crush. No one did.

Hmm ... Are you invited?

I knew I couldn't go, but still, I wanted him to invite me. Had he even noticed me?

Yeah.

The heat of jealousy raced up my neck to my cheeks.

You can come with me.

No — can't. Parents gone. Staying with D's
grandparents.

I looked up as Lynn started turning into a gravel driveway. "How long are we staying again?" I asked.

"We'll be back on Sunday night," Lynn said, as we approached a two story cottage with gray shingles. It nestled on a wide sloping lawn leading to a glass-like expanse of greenish-blue water.

Just as we turned in, I got another text. It was from Diana.

I'm going to invite Noah over.

I looked at her while she raised her eyebrows. I shook my head.

She texted me again.

Why not?

Noah and Diana had gotten to be best buddies. I didn't think he should come over while we were visiting with Grandpa and Grandma Roberts. I just didn't. But I couldn't think of a reason.

You say you don't like him like that.

Just then we came to the end of the driveway, and a big silver-haired man with a ruddy face came out of the side door, waving enthusiastically, using broad arm motions to direct Lynn where to park. He looked just the same as he did two years ago when I met him at Daddy and Lynn's wedding. His eyes and smile looked like Lynn's.

"He always tells me where to park," Lynn said under her breath to Daddy. "It's like I'm still learning how to drive."

"Now you know how I feel," Diana said.

"Oh, just roll with it." Daddy squeezed Lynn's arm.

Did he say that in a mad voice or a joking voice? Was that arm squeeze a sign of affection, or a sign of annoyance? I wished I could stop overanalyzing every little thing.

"Hi, Dad!" Lynn called as she climbed out of the car. She ran to him, and Grandpa Roberts enveloped her in a hug.

Then he started hugging everyone, even me. "Now let me give this beautiful young lady a hug, too," he said, and soon crushed me in his warm, muscular arms.

Grandma Roberts, a tiny white-haired lady, came out onto the porch. "There you are!" she cried. "I thought you would never get here!"

"But we're not late, Mom," Lynn said.

"I know, I was just so eager for you to come I hardly knew what to do with myself. Come on and eat lunch! I have food ready."

"I told you we wouldn't have time to eat," Lynn said.

"You have time for a little something."

"Norm and I have to get on the road. We have to check in this afternoon."

"At least you have time to come see the goose eggs we have down on our pontoon boat cover," said Grandpa Roberts. "There're seven of them. I think they're going to hatch any day now. And then we'll have little goslings!"

"Goslings?" asked Diana. "Cool!"

"Come in, come in," Grandma Roberts said. "Grandpa's early tomatoes are in, and I have some soup or you can just have tomato sandwiches."

Diana glanced at me and made a comical face. "I forgot to tell you about the tomatoes. The tomatoes that ate New York."

"Lynn and I can only stay a few minutes," Norm said. "We really appreciate you all keeping the kids."

"Oh, we love it!" exclaimed Grandpa Roberts.

There was no saying no. In a few minutes, we were sitting around Grandma Roberts' table eating tomato vegetable soup. Grandma Roberts said how pleased they were to have me here with them, and she laid her small, cool hand on my arm.

"Well, I just think every married couple needs to have a little time together," said Grandma Roberts. "I'm so glad you two are going away for a few days.

And don't you worry about the girls one bit, we are going to be fine, aren't we?"

I studied Daddy's face, then Lynn's. Had they told Grandpa and Grandma Roberts they were going to get marriage counseling? When they kept it a secret from us? Didn't they think we were old enough to understand . . . ?

"So, Stephanie, what do you say?" Grandpa Roberts saying my name brought me out of my daydream. "Can you waterski? Kneeboard?"

"No, sir." I felt confusion and a twinge of panic. What had I missed? I didn't dare even look at Daddy. I looked at my soup bowl. Daddy would think it was a fantastic idea for me to be an expert water skier when I came home from this weekend.

"Excellent!" Grandpa Roberts said jovially. "We'll go skiing late this afternoon, then, when the lake traffic has died down and the water is like glass. You'll pop right up and be skiing like nobody's business."

"Sounds great, Steph," said Daddy. "Isn't it great to have an experienced boat driver willing to take the time to teach you? Thanks, George."

My chest tightened. I knew it! I knew he would love the idea.

"We don't have to go today," Diana jumped in. I shot her a look of gratitude.

"Of course we do!" said Grandpa Roberts. "You girls

are going to have the time of your lives this weekend. We'll have you kneeboarding and slaloming and jumping the wake by Monday, Miss Stephanie. Why, when your parents come to get you, you won't even want to go home! In fact, you two just head on back home Sunday night, just leave them here."

My heart squeezed hard, like somebody was standing on my chest. I fake-laughed with everyone else just so I wouldn't cry.

"Dad," said Lynn, laughing. "When we get here on Sunday, we're going to want our kids back."

"Well," said Grandma Roberts. "You just may not get them."

Our good-byes felt rushed. My throat got dry, and my stomach started to hurt. Jumping the wake? Staying with grandparents who were practically strangers? Waiting for Daddy and Lynn to talk to Jon and Olivia about whether our lives would change? How was I going to survive this weekend?

Before I knew it, Daddy and Lynn backed out of the driveway. Their car rounded the bend and then drove out of sight. I had to set my jaw. Somebody who's fifteen shouldn't cry when her parents leave.

"Diana, Stephanie, come down to the dock and see the mother goose," Grandpa Roberts said. I felt so glad to have something to do that I ran through the grassy yard all the way to the dock.

I followed Diana and Grandpa Roberts out onto the long dock, looking through the slits between the wooden boards at the shifting brownish-green water a few feet below. The sun was shining and the surface of the lake sparkled in sweeping patterns, feathered by the wind. Some people drove by in a boat, waving. We waved back. The wake from their boat rippled toward us, gently vibrating the dock, and then lapped onto the shore.

At the end of the long dock floated a smaller dock and a boat slip with a metal roof. In that boat slip bobbed a pontoon boat with a canvas cover. In an indentation of the cover toward the front of the boat sat a Canada goose, with her full gray body and long dark neck and head, with white markings on her throat and chin. As we approached she lowered her head, opened her black beak, and hissed at us.

"She's sitting on seven eggs," said Grandpa Roberts. "She never leaves the nest. There's the male right there. He goes and gets food for her."

Sure enough, swimming just along the edge of the dock was a dark-headed goose a little bit bigger than the one on the nest. He gave us a searching look and swam in a wary circle, ruffling his wings.

"They're used to Grandma and me, and eventually they'll get used to you, too," Grandpa said. "But we're not going to be able to use the pontoon boat for awhile!"

Just then Grandma Roberts joined us with a plastic bag of bread in her hand. She tossed some small pieces to the male, which swam forward quickly, stuck his neck out, and gobbled them down.

"Can I feed the female?" Diana asked.

"Sure." Grandma Roberts handed Diana some bread, and she tossed it close to the female sitting on the eggs. The female ignored the bread at first. Then, cautiously, without moving her body, she stretched her neck to reach the morsel. She grasped it in her bill, jerked her head rapidly to gulp it down, then sat back upright, eyeing us with suspicion.

"Do you want to feed them, Stephanie?" Grandma asked.

"That's okay," I said.

"She's been sitting on the eggs for almost a month," said Grandma.

"Wow," Diana said. "I would be so excited if they hatched while we were here!"

"Geese mate for life," Grandpa Roberts added. "These same two geese have been coming back to lay their eggs right around here for years. But this is the first time they've chosen our boat cover as a nest!"

The geese never took their beady dark eyes off of us.

I could see just the edge of one of the eggs beneath the mother's gray feathery breast.

"How do geese know who to pick as their mate?" I asked. What did geese know about staying together that people didn't know?

"Haha, yeah, do they ever fight with each other?" Diana asked. She got what I was talking about.

"I see them try to attack anything that comes near the nest, but I haven't seen them fight with each other," said Grandpa Roberts.

"Yeah, wonder if geese ever have to get marriage counseling." I gave myself a high voice, pretending to be the female goose. "I am so sick of sitting on these eggs. I never get to go anywhere."

Now Diana joined in, pretending to be the male goose, using a low voice. "I've been getting food for her for three weeks. She never even said thank you."

Grandma Roberts gave us a sharp look, but Grandpa Roberts laughed. "Well, sometimes the male does sit on the eggs, in fact, to give the female a break. I've seen him do it."

"Aww, sweet," Diana said. She glanced at me and got out her phone and sent a text. My phone dinged. I opened it and it said:

> Wonder if the geese ever have to go talk to Jon and Olivia?

I smiled at her. It felt good to kind of joke about it with Diana in secret. It felt good to joke with Diana, period. Even though we made up after the whole "annn-i-mal" thing, I still sometimes got the feeling that Diana wished I wasn't there.

"Next summer Grandma Roberts and I will be celebrating our fiftieth anniversary," Grandpa said. "Can you imagine that? Fifty years together?"

"No," Diana said. "That sounds like forever."

I couldn't, either. Gosh, that was more than three times longer than my entire life. This spring, Colleen had a boyfriend named Clay for two months and that had seemed like a long time for high school.

"Do you all ever fight?" Diana asked.

"Oh, no!" said Grandpa Roberts jovially. "As long as I do exactly what Grandma tells me to do!" He put his arm around Grandma Roberts and laughed.

"Now, that's not true, George," said Grandma.

Another boat went by, and this time a boy was riding a kneeboard behind the boat. He swung out and jumped the wake with a splash just as he passed us. A rainbow-colored wall of water sprayed out beside him. The wake from the boat made our floating dock rock, and Grandpa Roberts took hold of Grandma Roberts' elbow to steady her. I thought that was so sweet.

"Yep, we'll have you jumping the wake just like that in no time at all, Miss Stephanie," said Grandpa.

5

DIANA

Stephanie and I lay out on the dock in our bathing suits, enjoying the way it rocked every time a boat came by. It was hot and the sun beat down on us. Stephanie rubbed suntan lotion on her legs, and the smell floated over. I loved that smell of summer.

Every so often I'd dive in the water to cool off. "Come on in!" I said to Stephanie, swimming up to the floating dock. "The fish that bite you are really small, and it barely hurts at all!" I loved teasing Stephanie.

"Fish bite you?" Stephanie's jaw dropped.

"Yeah, sometimes little ones will see a mole or a freckle and think it's food and swim up and bite it. Grandpa Roberts says they try to bite his nipples."

"I'm never getting in!"

"Okay, I'm just kidding."

"Diana! Are you kidding or not?" Stephanie stood up and put her hands on her hips. She was wearing a pink and white striped bikini that her mom had just given her. More guilt-offerings from her mom.

"It doesn't hurt," I said. "I swear."

"Are there any snakes?"

"Only one or two," I said, with a grin.

"Just stop, Diana!"

Finally Stephanie got so hot that she decided she had to come in, and she kind of tiptoed down the wooden stairs that led into the water. When she stepped onto the lake's muddy bottom, she let out a squeal.

"Diana! It's muddy!"

"What did you think, that it was concrete under there?"

"It's all squishy in between my toes." She made a face, and swam deeper and started to tread water. She stayed in the water for probably thirty seconds, a minute tops, and then climbed out.

I dove a few times, opening my eyes under water. Two little fish with black dots just behind their eyes floated up to me curiously, then darted away into the watery shadows. I turned a couple of flips underwater, which I love to do. Then I pulled myself up on the floating dock, letting the water stream off me and darken the gray wood surface.

The geese had adjusted to us being there. Occasionally they talked to each other, a soft honking. I tried honking at them to see if they'd honk back at me.

"It would be so cool if the geese hatched while we're here," I told Stephanie. "Did you see *Fly Away Home?* That's one of my favorite movies. The baby geese hatched while a girl was watching and they imprinted on her and followed her around in a line."

"Oh, yeah, they thought she was their mother?"

"Uh-huh, and then she learned to fly that glider plane that looked like a goose, and they followed her down the coast to the place where they were supposed to migrate."

"That was a great movie," Stephanie said.

"Hey, I'm going to text Noah and see if he can come over," I said, wrapping my towel around me. "Grandma and Grandpa Roberts won't mind."

"I think you have the hots for him," Stephanie said.

"I do not! We're just friends!"

"Ha. You know that I don't think you should invite him," Stephanie said.

"Why not? You're always so worried about stuff, Steph."

"All I know is, every single time I've gone along with one of your ideas, I've gotten in trouble!"

I started laughing. "I have gotten you in trouble a lot. Sorry!" I added, in a voice that I know didn't sound sorry at all. I didn't care what Stephanie said. I texted Noah.

> Hey, we r at the lake at my grandparents' house. Want to come up and go tubing?

He answered right away.

> *Sure. Got a wakeboard?*

> Just a kneeboard and skis. Bring one. When R U coming?

> *Not sure. Tomorrow?*

I texted back and gave him directions. Stephanie narrowed her eyes at me as I was texting.

"You just invited Noah, didn't you?"

I sat up straighter. "Yep."

"You are unbelievable!" she said. "It doesn't matter what I say, you're just going to do whatever you want."

"Yep." I lay on my towel and closed my eyes, letting the warm sun dry the lake water from my skin. Stephanie would just have to deal with Noah, that's all.

A few minutes later, Grandpa Roberts came down to the dock carrying a tray with slices of watermelon on it. "Hey, girls, how about some watermelon? Grandma cut some up just for you."

We sat on the wooden bench and ate the sweet cold watermelon, letting the pink juice drip on the dock. The sun dropped lower in the washed blue sky and we listened to the waves lapping against the pilings.

"Look, the boat traffic has calmed down," said Grandpa. "Ready to kneeboard, Diana?"

"Sure!" I said.

"Stephanie, are you ready to learn?" Grandpa Roberts asked.

Stephanie studied her feet. "No."

"Oh, come on! You know you want to be able to do it!" Grandpa leaned over and squeezed Stephanie's knee. Stephanie flinched.

I helped Grandpa take the cover off the ski boat. Then we went up to the house and from the storage porch retrieved the skis, the kneeboard, the ski vests, and the tow line, and brought them down and loaded them into the boat.

I knew Stephanie was scared, but I also knew that she would be proud of herself if she learned how to do it, so I didn't try to talk Grandpa out of making her. The blue Wellcraft started up with a putter, then a roar as Grandpa turned the key, and I hopped in.

"Come on, Stephanie!" I called over the sound of the engine. Gas from the boat had created coin-sized rainbow slicks of oil on the surface of the water behind us. Reluctantly, she climbed in, holding onto the windshield, and then curling up in one of the seats in the back.

Grandpa headed out to the middle of the cove, and then cut the engine.

"Hop in the water, Miss Diana," he said.

"Okay!" My heart raced. I put on the ski vest, then tossed the knee board into the water and dove after it. Out in the center of the cove the water was a deeper green, and felt cooler. I floated, holding onto the board, and then Grandpa tossed me the tow rope with the handle. Grabbing the handle, I lay on my stomach on the board. It had been awhile since I'd been knee boarding, and I might be a little rusty, but it was like riding a bike. You didn't forget how. And I wanted to show off for Stephanie.

"Straightening up," he called, and gave the boat a little gas to pull the line taut.

"Ready?"

"Ready!" I gave him the thumbs up signal.

He hit the motor and the boat leaped forward, pulling me up out of the water. Pressure tightened my shoulder muscles. As soon as I felt stable, I folded my knees up underneath me so I was kneeling on the board, and pulled the strap tight over the tops of my thighs. Grandpa looked back, gave me the thumbs up.

I was skimming on top of the water, whizzing past the docks, flying through the air!

"Yee-haw!" I stayed directly behind the boat for a little while, then leaned right and jumped the wake and landed in the smooth water outside the wake. After riding along beside the boat for a little while, I swung back to the left, and jumped both wakes. Let myself swing all the way up beside the left side of the boat.

The wind rushed by and I skimmed the gleaming surface of the water and the air was filled with the roar of the boat. I grinned my biggest grin at Stephanie, who was turned around watching me. Grandpa gave a lasso movement of his arm above his head, letting me know he was going to turn around, and I let the action of the turning boat swing me wide and I jumped both wakes again.

I leaned back and enjoyed the scenery as it flashed by. Houses and docks, groves of sun-dappled trees, the grassy shoreline. Then I did my best trick: I put the handle behind my back and twirled around, doing a 360, stopping to kneeboard backwards for a few seconds. Then I twirled around the other way. What a rush!

After five trips up and down the cove, I was out of breath and my shoulders and knees were shaking. I gave Grandpa the finger across the neck motion to tell him I was going to drop the line. Leaning back, I threw the rope high in the air, and felt myself sink down into the water.

Grandpa drove the boat around to pick me up, and I clambered up the ladder on the back of the boat.

"Whew!" I collapsed, shaking, water streaming everywhere, into the back seat and wrapped myself in a towel. "My muscles feel like jelly!" I saw Stephanie's face, though, and I knew I'd impressed her.

"That was some good knee boarding!" Grandpa said. "Great job!" He pointed at Stephanie. "Now it's your turn, big girl! Let's go. No time like the present."

I looked over at Stephanie and her face was white as a sheet.

6

STEPHANIE

I guess I wasn't going to get out of this. The ski vest felt wet and clammy when I put it on and fastened the clasps. My mouth just went completely dry.

Grandpa and Diana were both giving me instructions at the same time.

"When you get out there, lie on the board on your stomach," Diana said.

"I'll pull the boat up a little to draw the rope taut," Grandpa added.

Diana: "Get the handle positioned."

Grandpa: "I'll drive along really slowly so you can pull your knees up under yourself and get balanced."

Diana: "Right, just as you get going, pull your knees up and under so you're kneeling on the board. And then pull the strap tight over the tops of your thighs. Keep the handle centered. Got it?"

My ears were buzzing. What'd she just say? I looked back and forth as they both tried to tell me what to do. I felt like I couldn't breathe. Sit on my knees? Pull my knees or pull the strap? Balance? *Yeah, right!*

"Okay! Hop in the water!" Grandpa said.

I sat on the side of the boat as we bobbed there for a minute, taking a few deep breaths, telling myself to be calm. "Here goes," I said. I let myself slide in.

The water wasn't chilly, but my teeth were chattering anyway. The vest kept me riding high in the water. Diana threw the kneeboard onto the water's surface beside me, and it skimmed along the top.

"Grab it!" she yelled.

I swam over and got hold of it and struggled to pull myself halfway up the way I'd seen her do. Grandpa drove the boat around me, to drag the rope handle around to where I could reach it.

"Grab it!" he said as he drove by, but I didn't reach for it quickly enough and he had to drive around again.

"Sorry," I said. A little wave went in my mouth.

"No problem," yelled Grandpa. "Okay, now, you know what to do?"

I kept myself from yelling "No!" and just gave him a small nod.

"Ready?" Diana called.

I held my thumb up, the way I'd seen her do. Floating along there, holding onto the handle, watching the boat ahead of me, time seemed to stand still. A breeze threaded by my ear and a wave slapped the bottom of the kneeboard.

Grandpa straightened up the boat, pulling the line taut and dragging me through the water just a little. The muscles in my shoulders pulled tight. The boat took off.

And I was pulled right up and over the kneeboard, landing face first in the water, leaving it behind.

The boat dragged me for a few feet, with torrents of water hitting me in the face. Stinging, it went up my nose. And then I let go.

Just before I fell in, I saw the handle fly through the air and then bounce along on top of the water.

"She's down!" Diana shouted at Grandpa. He turned the boat around. I swam back to get the kneeboard. Grandpa brought me the rope.

And I tried again.

Up, and over the kneeboard. Dragging through the water, drinking half of the lake. Letting go.

Diana yelling, "She's down!"

And I tried again.

Up, and over the kneeboard. Dragging through the water, drinking half the lake. Letting go.

"You're going to get it this time," said Grandpa as he drove by to bring me the rope again.

I didn't want to try anymore. I'd swallowed a ton of water, my eyes were burning, and the muscles of my shoulders ached with exhaustion.

"You can do it!" Diana yelled at me from the back of the boat. "Come on, Stephanie!"

A wave slapped me in the face.

Grandpa drove up a little ways to pull the rope taut. "Ready?" he yelled.

I took a deep breath, bracing myself for another try.

"Ready," I said. And he hit the throttle and took off. As I started moving I pulled my knees up underneath me and tried to center myself. I was shaky and the water surface below the board felt slippery as ice, but I was up on my knees. Water churned over the board and out behind me. I was afraid to move, but knew I needed to put the strap over my thighs. Slowly, I reached forward to get the strap.

And the board slipped right out from under me. I fell.

Again.

Grandpa brought the boat around. I swam after the board.

"You were up!" Diana yelled, leaning over the side. "You were up for a few seconds! Next time you'll get it!"

"But I'm so tired," I said, as I bobbed along with my arms stretched over the board.

"Have you had it?" Grandpa said.

"Yeah."

"Okay." He cut the engine and he and Diana helped me climb back into the boat.

I fell into a seat in the back. My arms were shaking so hard and I was completely out of breath. I felt like such a failure.

"That was a good try, Steph," Diana said. "You almost had it."

"We'll try again another day," Grandpa said. "It's tiring trying to learn." I wrapped myself in a towel. I felt like a rag doll.

Pretty soon we were back at the dock, and Diana was running around helping Grandpa tie the boat up to the cleats on the sides of the boat slip. I was shaking so much I wasn't even sure I could get out of the boat and walk back to the land.

Grandpa helped me out and I sat on one of the benches on the standing dock, still trying to catch my breath.

"I wish I could've done it," I said as we headed slowly

up the walkway to the house. I was proud of myself for at least trying, though. Last year I wouldn't have.

"You'll get it next time," he assured me, putting his arm over my shoulder.

"Y'all take your showers, and we'll have dinner in just a few minutes!" Grandma Roberts said as we trooped into the house. "Don't drip all over my carpet, now."

The aroma of roast beef filled the kitchen. Rolls were lined on a cookie sheet ready to be warmed, potatoes were nestled in a casserole dish, and a big bowl with a tossed salad with ruby red chunks of fresh tomatoes stood beside it.

My stomach growled. I was starving!

The hot shower felt great on my tired muscles. Diana and I were sharing a room upstairs with white wicker furniture. A flowered bedspread covered a queen-sized bed and one of frilly white lace covered another single bed under the window.

"I love this room," I said to Diana, as we were getting dressed. A little green desk by the door had tiny drawers that were fun to open and close. "I recognize that painting," I said, pointing to a print of a thoughtful and wispy-haired girl in a blue dress holding a watering can. "That's a famous painting by Renoir. We studied that in art."

"Oh, yeah?" Diana said, staring at the painting.

"This room is where Mom and I stayed for six months after Mom and Dad separated. I was supposed to sleep in the twin bed but we slept together in the queen."

"Aw. That's sweet."

"Yeah. A couple of times Dad came here and pounded on the front door and yelled that he wanted to talk to Mom and no one would answer the door."

"Ooh, that must have been horrible," I said. What happened between my parents had been much more civilized. They had sent me to Grammy's house for two weeks one summer and when I got back everything had been decided.

"Yeah, hearing him yelling like that made me cry. I was in second grade."

"Ooh, yeah." I shivered, wrapping a towel around my wet hair. "Nothing like that would ever happen with Daddy and Lynn, do you think?" I could feel my chest tighten just thinking about it. A few seconds of silence crawled by. My thoughts careened from one possibility to the next. Was it happening with Diana, too? She acted like she didn't care, but I wasn't sure I believed her.

Finally Diana shrugged. "I don't know. I'm never getting married, that's all I can say."

"Really?" I wasn't surprised to hear her say that, to tell the truth. "Why not?"

"Getting along with another person all the time is just too hard."

"But wouldn't you get lonely? I can see that marriage is hard, but I don't want to be alone." I ran a brush through my hair. "What about having kids?"

"I like being by myself," Diana said. "When I grow up I'm just going to have lots of pets. I'll have, like, seven dogs and five cats. They'll be my kids!"

I stood in front of the mirror in the bathroom, brushing my hair, thinking about what Diana had said. I pictured her living in a house with all those animals. "So, how do you think things are going with Jon and Olivia so far?"

"*Jon* and *Olivia*," said Diana, laughing. "Aren't you curious what they might be talking about? I bet they're talking about us, don't you?"

I laughed uneasily. "Yeah, probably."

"I mean, when I see Dr. Shrink, I talk about Mom and Norm sometimes."

"And me?"

Diana grinned. "Yeah, sometimes about you."

"I kind of wonder what it's like talking to a shrink. I mean, do you just talk?"

"Yeah. Mostly. I'll tell her about stuff that happens. Sometimes she'll ask questions and that's a pain because they're hard to answer."

"Questions about your feelings?"

"Yeah. Sometimes she'll make suggestions for ways for me to try to be more patient and calm down."

"I think that would be kind of cool," I said. "Is it?"

Diana shrugged. "Sometimes it's a pain."

All of a sudden my phone rang with Mama's ringtone, the theme song from "Mamma Mia," which she had picked herself. I set my jaw. I wasn't going to answer it. Then, after a few seconds, I broke down.

"Hi, sugar!" She sounded excited and out of breath. "Listen, I know you're mad at me because you've been ignoring my texts. But don't hang up, sugar. I felt so guilty about you not staying with me this weekend that I told Barry I couldn't meet him in Asheville. I'm here, and I want to come get you. I have to pick up Matt from work, since he lost his license, but I can come get you after that."

I got goosebumps all over. Mama had changed her plans for me! I didn't think she'd ever do that. "Wow," I said, not sure what to say. "That's kinda sudden, isn't it, Mama? I mean, are you sure?"

"I'm sure, sugar! We'll go shopping and get pedicures together tomorrow or something. I have to pick Matt up at eight, and then I can come get you. Just tell them I'm coming! Bye!"

I hung up, kind of stunned.

"What was that?" Diana asked.

"This kind of strange phone call from Mama. She

said she changed her plans and I can stay with her this weekend and she's coming to get me later tonight."

"She's coming to get you?" Diana plopped down on the bed with a disappointed look on her face. "Don't go! Do you want to go?"

I couldn't answer her. I truly didn't know. I had felt kind of awkward when I first got here, but Grandma and Grandpa Roberts had made me feel really welcome. I'd been mad at Mama, but now she'd changed her plans for me. I wanted to be with Mama, but what about Matt? Would he be around this weekend? Even though he'd been nicer to me, I still hadn't forgotten the times he'd been mean, and once even threatened me.

"You've got to stay, Steph! When Noah comes you won't be able to hang out. And you won't learn to kneeboard."

I didn't look at her. Instead, I went around the room, gathering my hair dryer and overnight case and wet bathing suit and putting them back into my suitcase. I didn't know what I wanted. I didn't like being mad at Mama. I wanted things between us to be good.

"Dinner's ready! Come and eat!" Grandma called from downstairs.

Trying to kneeboard works up an appetite. The salad was laden with Grandpa's juicy tomatoes, and the roast, potatoes, and hot bread all smelled fantastic.

"That was a good try out on the kneeboard today,

Stephanie," Grandpa said. "I'm sure you'll get it next time you try."

"I hope so," I said. I felt like such a dork. I bet Diana had gotten up on her first try.

"Well, let's talk about our plans for tomorrow," said Grandma. "Diana, you're working at the horse barn and we need to get you there, is that right?"

"Right, I have to be there at eight," Diana said, slathering margarine onto her potato. She looked over at me. "I hope Commanche's hoof is better."

I waited for Diana to mention the fact that she had invited Noah to the lake, but she didn't.

"And Stephanie, you have to teach two gymnastics classes tomorrow morning, right?" Grandma added.

I knew now it was time for me to tell Grandma and Grandpa Roberts that Mama was coming. I bit into my bread, hesitating. I was afraid they might get mad. But then Diana did it for me.

"Stephanie's mom is coming to get her tonight," Diana told them.

Grandma put down her fork. "She is? I thought you were supposed to be here for the whole weekend."

"I was, but Mama changed her plans and I can stay with her now. She's not going to Asheville to meet Barry."

"But you have to learn to kneeboard!" said Grandpa.

"Oh," said Grandma with a sigh. "It's been so nice to have you with us. I wish you could stay."

I felt myself blushing. They were being so kind. I didn't know what to do.

I wished none of this had ever happened. That Daddy and Lynn hadn't gone away. That Mama hadn't had other plans when we called her. That Mama and I had never had a fight. I really wasn't sure what I wanted to do.

After dinner, Diana and I helped Grandma with the dishes, then ran up to our room to get our flip-flops se we could go with Grandpa to the movie store. On our way back down, Diana grabbed my hand and we stopped in the middle of the stairs. She put her finger to her lips and we listened.

"Do you think the girls know why Lynn and Norm went away?" Grandma was saying. Dishes clattered as she finished loading the dishwasher.

"I don't know, why?" asked Grandpa.

"Well, Lynn said they didn't tell them, but what did you think about what they said out on the dock this afternoon, when they were pretending to be the male and female goose getting marriage counseling?" asked Grandma.

"Oh, that? You think that proves that they know about it?"

"It aroused my suspicions. Why would the girls say something like that otherwise?"

"You've got a point. Maybe they've figured it out."

"I just don't like those girls having to face so much uncertainty. That's one reason why I don't want Stephanie to go with her mother tonight. They've already had enough disruption in their lives. They don't need more."

"Well, it's her mother," Grandpa said.

There was silence. Diana looked at me and nodded, and we continued down the stairs. My heart pounded in my chest. Grandma and Grandpa did know about where Daddy and Lynn had gone! Would there be a big argument when Mama got here?

Diana, who is better than I am at faking things, pretended we hadn't heard anything. She immediately talked Grandpa into letting her drive to the movie store, so she climbed into the drivers' seat, Grandpa rode shotgun, and I climbed into the back of their sedan. Diana had a little trouble backing out of the long driveway, and I turned and watched out the rear window, thinking about how I would be learning to do this myself next year.

"Slow down, now," Grandpa told her as she drove down their street. "This is a winding road and you don't want to take these corners too fast."

"Okay." She slowed down a little. Diana didn't talk back to Grandpa the way she talked back to Lynn.

On the way home, after getting a movie, dusk was approaching, and Grandpa made Diana turn on the headlights. As we turned back onto Grandpa and Grandma's street, and began the winding descent down to the lake, Grandpa said, "Well, Diana, you did a pretty good job driving other than being a bit aggressive with the accelerator. When your mother learned to drive a stick shift, I believe my hair turned white in one day."

Diana laughed. "That's pretty funny."

We were all laughing when we came around the last turn. And, that was when it happened. Suddenly, out of nowhere, a deer leaped right in front of our car. Its narrow head, with large frightened eyes, soared directly in front of our windshield.

"Look out!" yelled Grandpa Roberts.

"Oh!" Diana yelled slamming on the brakes.

The deer's long, powerful front legs hit the road directly in front of our right tire, and then we slammed with a loud thump into the deer's shoulder.

I screamed.

7

DIANA

"I couldn't help it! It jumped right out in front of me!"
I burst into tears.

"Just pull over to the side of the road," Grandpa said.

But I was shaking all over. I couldn't move. I had hit a deer! A beautiful deer! I sat there frozen and sobbing, with the engine running. Over and over in my head, I kept hearing the sound of that thump.

Finally, Grandpa got out and walked around to the driver's side. "Can you slide over, honey? Let me pull the car over."

I managed to move over to the passenger seat. "What happened to it?"

"I don't know. That's what we're going to see," Grandpa said. He slid behind the wheel and pulled the car over to the side of the road.

"I'm going to look for the deer," he said, cutting the engine. "You girls stay here."

"No, I'm coming with you!" I said.

"No, if it's hurt I don't want you to see it," Grandpa said.

But I didn't listen. Still shaking like crazy, with tears rolling down my cheeks, I jumped out of the car and followed Grandpa into the wooded area beside the road. Even though we had hit the deer, it hadn't fallen down. It had just kept on running. And it was nowhere to be seen. Grandpa and I tromped through the branches and underbrush, searching through climbing vines and under pine trees, combing the area for fifty yards around, while Stephanie waited in the back seat of the car. We couldn't find it.

Finally Grandpa said, "It must have been okay. It didn't stop. Maybe it wasn't that badly hurt."

"That thump sounded so awful, Grandpa." Tears started leaking again from the edges of my eyes just thinking about it. "Do you think if I had been a more experienced driver I could have done anything?"

"No, it jumped out directly in front of us, honey,"

Grandpa said. "There was absolutely nothing you could do. If I had been driving, I would have hit that deer."

Still I was shaking.

Grandpa stopped to examine the car when we got back. The right front headlight was smashed. "Well, it's a good thing it's not any worse," he said.

"Did you find the deer?" Stephanie asked when we climbed into the car.

"No, it completely disappeared," I told her. "So maybe I didn't really hurt it."

"Just no way of knowing," Grandpa said as he started the car and headed back down the road. "You know, when living things have the fight or flight response, they have a lot of adrenalin running through their system, so they can do some amazing things, even with serious injuries. We'll probably never know what happened to that deer."

After we told Grandma about hitting the deer, I went upstairs and got into the bed and pulled the flowered bedspread up over my head. I felt horrible. I had seen the deer's beautiful face just as we hit it, with its terrified eyes. I could close my eyes and feel the thudding jolt as we hit.

For school I had just read *The Yearling*, the story about a boy who raised a deer. I had loved reading about the way the boy related to the deer, all the deer's antics inside the house, and the deer's funny and mischievous personality. The boy had named the deer Flag. But the boy's life was very hard, and the story had been so sad in parts.

Stephanie and Grandma Roberts came upstairs after me. "Maybe the deer will be all right," Stephanie said, sitting on the side of the bed.

"I'm never driving again," I said, from under the bedspread.

"Oh, nonsense," Grandma Roberts said. "Grandpa told me the deer ran right out in front of you. There was nothing you could do. It wasn't your fault."

"Why do animals do that, anyway? Run out in front of cars?" I asked, folding the bedspread back so I could see them.

"Well, you know, they might be confused by the lights," Grandma said. "They may be scared but not know which way to run."

"I'm not driving anymore," I repeated. I had been so excited about getting my license, but right now the idea of getting behind the wheel just made me start shaking again, just like Stephanie. I was pathetic. I might have killed a living thing. I might be a murderer.

A minute later, a knock sounded on the front door downstairs.

"That's probably Mama," Stephanie said. She went

over to the twin bed and slung her weekend bag over her shoulder.

"Oh, no, we're not ready for you to leave, Stephanie!" Grandma said.

We heard Grandpa downstairs answering the door. "Well, hello, come in, come in," he said.

"Hey there," came Stephanie's mom's voice. "Thanks so much for keeping my Stephanie today."

Stephanie headed downstairs and Grandma Roberts and I followed her. Stephanie's mom, normally with perfect hair and makeup, had mascara smears and bags under her eyes. She looked like she'd been crying. She was talking and waving her hands around nervously. "I appreciate you keeping Stephanie but I can keep her now."

"Hey, Mama," Stephanie said.

Her mom pulled her close and wrapped her arms around her. "Hey, sugar!"

"We were expecting to have Stephanie all weekend," said Grandma Roberts. "We were looking forward to it."

"I know, and I so appreciate you being willing to keep her, but my plans have changed." Stephanie's mom was playing with Stephanie's hair now, picking it up and smoothing it down over her shoulder.

"All right, then," said Grandma Roberts. "We'll miss you, Stephanie."

Stephanie's mother pulled her more tightly against her, wrapping her arms around her neck.

I looked at Stephanie's face. She looked uncomfortable and a little scared.

"Where's Matt?" I asked.

"He's out waiting in the car. I just picked him up from his job at the carwash. We're all going to head home and have a nice time together."

"How is Matt getting along since his accident?" asked Grandma Roberts.

"Really well," said Stephanie's mom. "He regained all the movement in his arm, and he's got that carwash job, and he'll be taking classes at the community college this summer, too. He's really turned over a new leaf. We're proud of him."

"That's wonderful," said Grandma Roberts.

"Well, sugar, if that's all your stuff, let's get going," said Stephanie's mom. "Thanks again."

"Thanks for having me," said Stephanie. "Thanks for dinner and for the kneeboarding lesson." I looked at her face and the expression was hard to read.

"Our pleasure," Grandpa Roberts boomed. "And we want you to come back again."

"Any time," said Grandma Roberts, and she lay her hand on Stephanie's arm.

"Bye," Stephanie said to me. "I guess I'll see you back at home next week."

But would she? What was going to happen when Mom and Norm got home?

"Bye," I said. "Text me."

"Yeah, okay, I will."

I went outside on the front porch to watch as Stephanie walked up the long driveway to her mom's car. Matt, sitting in the front passenger seat, waved. After a second, I waved back.

I lay on the couch in the family room of the lake house. It wasn't going to be any fun to watch the movie without Stephanie.

"I don't feel good about letting that girl go tonight," said Grandma Roberts. She sat at the end of the couch and put my feet in her lap.

Grandpa sat down in his La-Z-Boy. "Well, it's too late now. She's gone."

"Did you think it looked like her mother had been crying?"

"Yes," I said.

"You thought so, too?"

I nodded.

"What's her husband like, do you know, Diana?"

"I don't know." I thought about Barry. "He's tall."

"Well, that doesn't tell me much!"

"He's a pilot. He likes golf."

"But what's he like?"

"I don't know, Grandma! I never paid much attention to him. I've only met him once or twice. He's not usually around." Sometimes Grandma asked a lot of questions.

"Hmmm," said Grandma.

"It's all right. Nothing to worry about. It's good for her to be with her mom," said Grandpa. "Now, who wants some popcorn with the movie?"

"I don't feel like watching the movie now," I said. "Stephanie's gone. And I hit a deer." And Mom and Norm are fighting, but I kept that thought to myself.

"Nonsense," said Grandpa. "This too shall pass."

He was always saying that.

Later, in my bed in the white wicker bedroom I lay in the dark and listened to the crickets singing outside. It was a soothing sound. I wondered how Stephanie was doing with her mom and if she could hear crickets too.

8

STEPHANIE

I didn't know if Barry had gone to Asheville by himself or not. All I knew was he wasn't at Mama's house when we got there. Right away Matt went to his room and shut the door.

I sat in the family room with Mama and we watched some singing show that she had taped. I leaned up against her and she scratched my head the way she always does. Her phone dinged a few times, telling her she had texts, but she didn't look at them. Once I said,

"If you want to talk to Barry, go ahead, don't worry about me," but she just shook her head.

At one point, Matt trooped down the stairs and went in the kitchen to get a snack, making a bunch of noise. He was on the phone arguing with a friend about whether the greatest quarterback of all time was John Elway or Tom Brady. Then, he surprised me by coming out into the family room to eat his bowl of cereal.

"I know a guy who auditioned in Charlotte for *American Idol*," he said in between mouthfuls.

"Really?" Mama said. Using the remote, she paused the show while we talked.

"Yeah. He said he had to wait in line for hours," he said. "And his audition lasted about fifteen seconds. He didn't make it."

"Oh, too bad. What did he sing?" Mama asked.

"Um ... some song by John Mayer, I think."

"Did any of the judges say mean things to him?" I asked.

"No, he said they were nice. They said to keep practicing and come back next year."

"It must've been an amazing experience," Mama said.

"A lot of waiting," Matt said. "But he said everyone waiting in line started singing together, which was cool. And they had people with cameras coming around and you were supposed to shout 'I'm the next American Idol!' "

"That sounds fun," I said.

Mama pressed the remote, and the show started again.

Matt sat with us and watched a girl sing, and then joked, "Well, you know, that was a little pitchy," imitating one of the judges. He started laughing.

I laughed, too. Matt was making an effort to talk to us, and he never used to do that before.

"So, I have to be at the carwash tomorrow by nine," he said to Mama. Because of his accident, Matt lost his driver's license for six months, and Barry and Mama and some of his friends have had to drive him around.

"Okay," she said.

"Okay. Later." And then he went back upstairs, leaving his empty bowl sitting on the coffee table.

After the show was over, I thought Mama would want to sit and talk. I had planned to tell her about trying to kneeboard. But she yawned and stretched and told me she was tired, so we went to bed.

I had a hard time getting to sleep. I texted Diana.

R u ok after the deer?

I guess. How's Matt?

Being nice! Can u believe it?

No!

Mama is acting weird. Not talking as much.

What's up with that?

*Don't know. What do u think is going on with
Daddy and Lynn?*

Don't know.

Should we call or text them?

No.

Wonder what they've told Jon and Olivia?

No idea. Remember when Norm got mad at the
ranch when I refused to go rafting?

*And how mad Daddy was when we had the fight in
the car over ur phone? Do u think they're telling
Jon and Olivia stuff like that?*

I hope not! It's so embarrassing!

*I think it's about Daddy not going to Florida. And
Lynn having to chaperone my cheerleading
competition.*

I was always feeling guilty about things, and I told
myself I wasn't going to feel guilty about that.

If they split up, where would you live?

Goose bumps ran from my backbone up to my skull and spread all over my scalp, prickling. I started to feel like I had to throw up. It was obvious that Diana would still be with Lynn. I couldn't answer. After a minute, Diana texted me again.

> Mr. Goose never lets me pick the place for the nest.

I smiled. She could tell that I was upset and was trying to joke around a little.

With relief, I answered.

> *Mrs. Goose always has to be first when we swim with the babies.*

Diana texted back.

> If the baby geese hatch u'll miss it.

> *I know.*

She was so predictable. I was sitting here worrying about Daddy and Lynn, but there was Diana, thinking about what was happening with the animals.

9

DIANA

The next morning Grandpa got me up early to go to the barn. He tried to persuade me to practice my driving on the way over, but I was still thinking about hitting the deer.

"As they say, you've got to get back on the horse," Grandpa said. But he didn't pressure me, and he got in the driver's seat.

As we drove down the street, past the spot where I'd hit the deer last night, the whole scene played out in my head again. The beautiful narrow head. The big startled eyes. The strong long legs. And the jarring thud. I glanced through the woods around the road, looking for a deer streaking through the dappled sunlit leaves. I thought about the deer maybe limping through the woods, or lying on its side, trying to get up. I remembered the time I'd been searching for the lost wolves, and found Waya lying on her side in the woods, shot.

"Do you think I killed the deer, Grandpa?" I asked again.

Grandpa patted my knee. "Sweetheart, I don't think we'll ever know. It was an accident. You know how the saying goes ..."

"I know, I know. 'This too shall pass.'"

I tried pushing the memory of it out of my mind. Noah had texted me this morning, saying he would come over this afternoon and bring his own wakeboard. He had asked if Grandpa would be able to drive the boat for him and I said "yes." I hadn't mentioned it to Grandma or Grandpa, yet, though. I thought maybe I would mention it when we got home from the barn. Or maybe I'd just let him show up. That way Grandma and Grandpa couldn't say no.

"I wonder how things are going with Stephanie and her mom," I said.

"I bet everything is fine," Grandpa said reassuringly. "Tell me about what you do at the barn."

"Josie, who's in charge of the barn, lets me muck stalls and fill water troughs and clean tack in exchange for some of my riding time with Commanche."

Grandpa took the ramp to the highway to head for Charlotte. "So Commanche is the horse you ride?"

"For the last few years, yeah. He's my buddy. He always sticks his head out of his stall when he hears me coming."

"So you have a special relationship with him."

"Yeah. He's got a sore hoof right now, so I'll just be helping him soak his foot. I won't be able to ride him today."

The barn stood at the end of a long, winding driveway. Grandpa parked on the side and then walked in with me. It was a red, open barn with bands of sunlight streaming through the open front and back doors. Josie was sweeping the floor when we walked in, and the particles she swept up seemed to sparkle in the sunbeams.

"You ready to get to work?" Josie asked, after I introduced Grandpa. "Got a lot to do today. We need to turn the horses out and pick the stalls. We also need to groom the horses, put sunscreen on their noses, and spray them with fly spray."

"Put sunscreen on their noses?" asked Grandpa.

"Oh, yes, horses with white noses can get sunburned," Josie said.

"How's Commanche?" I headed over to his stall and peeked in. He was standing facing the back wall, favoring his leg, and barely turned his head when I came up. Usually he came to the stall door and let me pet his head and neck.

"Oh, he's a grumpy bear," Josie said. "And you're going to have to soak that foot again today."

Grandpa came over to Commanche's stall and peered in. "Poor fella," he said.

"Hey, Grandpa, before you leave, I want you to see something," I said. "Come back here."

A Clydesdale, with heavy fur from his knees to his hooves, hung his gigantic head over the top of a metal gate separating the barn from the back paddock. Beside him, a miniature donkey the size of a large dog poked his nose through the metal strips of the gate. They looked so funny standing there together, the giant and the pygmy.

"This is David and Goliath," I said, giving the miniature donkey a quick scratch on his head. "They're best friends. They're inseparable. When it rains, David stands underneath Goliath so he won't get wet. Isn't that funny?"

"How about that," said Grandpa, with a laugh. "Unlikely friends."

"Sorta like me and Steph," I said. As if on cue, the

donkey, David, swung his little head around and nuzzled Goliath's knee.

"Aww!" I said. "Horses are always picking out a best friend. It's cool."

"How about that? I wonder how they pick each other?" Grandpa squeezed my shoulder. "Be back to get you in a couple of hours, okay?"

As soon as he left, I checked Josie's white board, where she'd assigned each of us "barn rats" our individual chores.

Time at the barn flew by and the sun rose higher in the sky. After I cleaned the other stalls, I filled the bucket with warm water and went see Commanche.

"Hey, buddy, we gotta do this." I whispered encouragement as I lifted his hoof and submerged it into the water. Then I poured in the Epsom salts and let them dissolve.

He shook his head, blowing air through his nostrils. I sat on the floor next to his leg,

"That should feel pretty good, buddy," I said.

His ear cocked back in my direction. He shifted his weight.

Then he butted me with his nose to say hello.

"So ... not grumpy anymore, huh?" I said.

Later, while I was grooming him, he swished his tail contentedly. I made sure I showed him each brush before I used it on him, so he'd know what to expect.

He nuzzled my pockets for treats, because I always brought them for him, and I gave him some carrots I'd gotten from Grandma. I stood grooming him, inhaling his horsey smell, and stroking his smooth, solid neck. Worries about everything else flew out of my mind. I didn't think, I just was.

10

STEPHANIE

This morning Mama took Matt back to work at the carwash, and he said he'd have no problem getting a ride home. Then she took me to teach my tumbling classes. Those little kids always put me in a good mood. They're always saying, "Miss Stephanie, watch me, watch me!" and showing me what they've learned to do. They're so limber and full of energy and they crawl all over me like puppies. It makes me feel really good. At the end of class I let them jump around in the pit and they love that. They're like a bunch of little jumping beans. There's a boy in my class who reminds me of a frog, the way he jumps around.

Now Mama and I sat side by side with our feet in warm whirling baths at a nail salon, while two chattering Asian girls massaged them. I'd never had a pedicure before! Mama got them all the time but this was the first time she'd brought me along. Colleen said her older sister had one before she went to the prom, and it was fantastic. It was true! I couldn't believe Mama had done this. It wasn't a special occasion or anything.

Right when we walked in, a dark-eyed girl showed us a wall of polishes, where row upon row of beautiful rainbow bottles stood lined on small shelves. They were in every possible color and shade. I stood there staring. How to decide?

I picked a pale pink polish.

"Oh, sugar, can't you be more adventurous than that?" Mama said. She picked purple. Right away I felt bad about my choice, but I stuck with it. I felt weird having these girls wait on me, but I was kind of sore from trying to kneeboard yesterday and the girl's strong hands felt so good as she kneaded my feet – my toes, the balls of my feet, my arches, my heels, and around my ankles. I was so relaxed I felt like sinking right through the chair.

The girls massaging our feet were talking to each other in another language. My girl, the one with long hair, seemed like she was telling a story to Mama's girl, with short hair. My girl seemed upset about something, and Mama's girl seemed like she was being supportive. I wondered what the story was about.

I glanced over at Mama. The water bubbled around her feet and she had one hand curled over her brow, so I couldn't see her face. She was reading a text. I felt like something was bothering Mama. I didn't know what to do, but I wished I could help.

Thirty minutes later, I wiggled my toes, waiting for the polish to dry. The polish was so shiny! We had these little strips of plastic wound between our toes to keep them separated. Mama had paid and tipped the girls who helped us and she was flipping through a magazine, looking at the ads.

I had nothing really to do so I watched the two Asian girls with their next customers, still talking to each other. I was glad that they were such good friends. It reminded me of Diana, so I texted her.

Hey, just got my first pedi!

And she texted back, Cool! What color?

Pale pink.

LOL. Predictable.

On the way to the mall Mama put the top down in her car and we drove with the wind blowing all around, and then she turned on the radio really loud and we sang at the top of our lungs. It was really nice to have Mama to myself.

Inside the mall, I picked out a few things to try on. Mama said she liked everything I tried on, and offered to buy anything I wanted. But I could tell something was still bothering her. She kept checking her phone. While we were standing in line to check out, I just asked her, "Mama, is anything wrong?"

She used to talk to me about her feelings of loneliness after the divorce, and when she introduced Barry to me, she said, "I really, really want you to like him, sugar." Lately she hadn't talked as much. When I spent time with Mama, I often felt like I was trying and trying to understand what was going on with her, but I never could.

"Are you glad I didn't go to Asheville?" she asked me.

"Yes!" I said, and I made sure my voice sounded enthusiastic. "I'm so glad I was able to stay with you this weekend and get a pedicure and come shopping and everything."

"And maybe we'll eat dinner at the Cheesecake Factory, how about that?" she said.

"I love the Cheesecake Factory!" I said.

"We'll go there, then," she said, squeezing my arm. Her phone dinged, and she glanced at it.

"Mom," I said. "What's going on?"

All of a sudden tears sprang to her eyes. "Stephanie ... I decided to make a stand this weekend. And ... I think what I did does matter. It did make a difference."

"What do you mean?"

"The other day you said that I always choose Barry, and this time I didn't. I chose you."

I stared at her. I knew I should never have said what I said the other day about her choosing Barry.

"The thing is, Sugar, Barry still wants me to come up. He's waiting for me. The important thing is that he understands that you and I needed some time together, so this was good. " Tears rolled down her cheeks, and she quickly swiped them away.

"Was?" I asked. Everything about this day had seemed strange. Almost like a movie or a play, everything staged.

Mama looked at her watch. "If I leave for Asheville after we go to the Cheesecake Factory, I can get there before midnight." She wrapped the fingers of one hand around the muscle of her upper arm and squeezed. "You and Matt are getting along okay these days, aren't you? I mean, is there anything else you wanted to do this weekend? You'll be all right. I mean, gosh, you babysit, of course you'll be all right."

I stared at her. My breath caught in my throat, and my eyes began to sting. She was going to leave. After coming to pick me up last night, she was going to leave me with Matt and go meet Barry.

11

DIANA

I tied my running shoes tightly and did some stretches
on the front porch steps.

"Don't go too far!" Grandma Roberts called, through
the screened door. "I don't want you getting lost, now!"

"I'm not going to get lost," I said. Their street made a
big loop along the lakefront, so all I had to do was keep
running and I'd be back home. Sometimes Grandma
Roberts worried too much.

I took off to the left and headed down a small hill.
A jumble of thoughts flashed through my mind.

Stephanie thought there was something going on between Noah and me. What would it be like if Noah and I got together?

Did I have a crush on Noah, and I just wasn't admitting it?

Hot pink roses were in full bloom beside mailboxes and in yards. Stark white flowers with a strong perfumey smell bloomed on bushes with dark shiny leaves. Houses lined the lake side of the road, but on the other side stretched acre after acre of piney woods. Occasional patches of sunlight filtered through the branches. I let my gaze wander through the shadowed underbrush in between the trees. In those woods somewhere was there an injured deer, or one that had died, because of me?

I tried to push the thought out of my head. Grandpa Roberts had said the only thing to do was go forward. His saying came back to me. "This too shall pass." I smiled to myself.

Heat radiated from the dark asphalt. I pounded the road, my breath coming in sharp staccato bursts.

My thoughts came back to Mom and Norm. Stephanie was really worried. She didn't even know who she'd live with if they split up. I had gotten used to our family. I liked the four of us together. I still had my issues with Norm. I still wasn't sold on the idea of going to church. I didn't know where I was in my relationship with God. My nonexistent relationship with God. But as for Stephanie, I had to admit that now I liked having her to talk to about stuff. Even after all our fighting.

Was it me that was causing the problem for Mom and Norm? Stephanie said she thought that Norm not going to Florida to see her cheerleading competition was what did it. But I bet that wasn't really it. I bet it was me. I was a pain. I was high-maintenance. I was hard to get along with. I was making Mom have to make choices between me and Norm.

Well, she should choose me, shouldn't she? I was her daughter. I should come first. A mother should choose her child before her husband. Shouldn't she?

Did I want Mom to have to pick Norm or me?

The road led uphill, and the muscles on the backs of my legs strained. I tried to breathe with the rhythm of my strides. Three steps breathing in, two steps breathing out.

I followed the road to the right, circling back toward the house. Through the yards of the houses on my right, I could see the bright flashes of the lake just beyond.

Stephanie and I were going to have to do something. Something to keep Mom and Norm together. Convince them that they didn't have to choose. But what would that be?

My jumbled thoughts began to smooth out. It always happened when I went for a run. Problems that seemed insurmountable somehow became solvable. Just making it to the end of the run became my main goal, and when I managed that, everything else seemed a little easier, too.

I was coming to the last stretch of lakefront homes on my left and piney woods on my right. Right near where I had hit the deer. I glanced at a sunlit patch in the woods and saw a flash.

What was that? Something had moved! I ran a few more steps then stopped and went back. I peered down toward a patch of dappled underbrush right beside a cone of sunlight. I couldn't really see.

Had I imagined it? It seemed like something small was moving in there. I left the road and headed through the pine needles, my footsteps quiet and silky-sounding. The green pine boughs brushed my arms as I wound my way through, and the air became cooler in the shadows.

A low-hanging bush trembled. And before I knew it, right there in front of me, a spindly little thing was rising unsteadily to its feet and bleating.

It came right up to me! Reaching out with its round black nose. It sounded like it was saying, "Maa! Maa!" The most beautiful little white-spotted fawn that you've ever seen — long slim legs, a long narrow muzzle, creamy white throat, big pear-shaped ears, and the biggest brown eyes, with long straight lashes.

"Maa! Maa!" It was coming towards me! Trying to talk to me, stomping its little hooves, asking me for something.

I could reach out and touch it! This was so amazing, my hands were shaking!

With slow, trembling fingers, I touched the fawn's head. It didn't try to run away. Then I ran my palm over its narrow little head and down its neck. The fur was soft, like a short-haired dog's. It kept bleating, touching its cold wet nose to me. It was smaller than I had imagined a fawn to be. No taller than a cat. It must be really young.

It had the most beautiful row of white markings that started right along its backbone and speckled its sides like stars. I decided it was a girl and that I'd name her Star.

What did she want? She acted hungry. Where was her mother? Surely she would be nearby. Surely she hadn't abandoned her baby.

I looked around trying to see through surrounding tree trunks in all directions.

The fawn bleated again. I took a step away, and she followed me.

I knelt beside her and petted her small, delicate head.

"Hey, what's going on?" I said in a soft voice. "Are you hungry? Where's your mom? Did she leave you here?"

Her ears were so sensitive, twitching this way and that.

Reaching gently around her little body, I picked her up, letting her legs hang down. She was so small, so light. I could feel her little heart beating frantically, and she struggled to escape, her hooves jamming into my arms, but I had a tight hold on her.

I ran home, carrying her in my arms, feeling her soft fur and musky smell next to my T-shirt. She was bleating and trying to kick me with her tiny little hooves, but I tore down the driveway and up the porch steps.

I kicked at the screened door. "Grandma! Grandpa! I found a fawn!"

Grandma came to the door, and her hand flew to her mouth. "Oh, my goodness!"

Grandpa was standing right behind her. "Good night, Miss Agnes!"

"I found her in the woods," I said. "I didn't see her mother anywhere. She's hungry. Do you know what to feed a fawn?"

"Shouldn't you have just left her there? Maybe her mother is coming back to get her," Grandma said.

In *The Yearling*, the mother deer had been shot. The mother didn't ever come back for that fawn.

"Maybe the mother isn't coming back. We need to

feed her." I held her tight to my chest. "Can I bring her inside?"

"A wild animal in this house? I should say not!" said Grandma.

"Please?"

"Maybe on the sun porch," Grandpa suggested.

"Well, don't bring it through the house!" said Grandma.

I carried the fawn around back and Grandpa opened the door to the sun porch. I brought her in and put her down. She stood uncertainly, in amongst our ski vests and boating equipment, bleating again. She was the most adorable thing I'd ever seen in my life. Everything about her was tiny, from her rounded hooves to the white star-like spots on her sides. She hardly seemed real.

"I named her Star," I told Grandpa.

"Maybe you should have put her back for her mother to find." Grandpa ran his hand over her back, and she bleated again. "I guess we better go online and find out what to feed her," he said.

I knelt beside Star and ran my hand over her bony little backbone. Oh, she was so cute and helpless. She needed me. She stood uncertainly for a moment, staring at me, and then she tottered over to the window and touched her nose to the glass.

Meanwhile Grandpa brought his laptop out onto the

sun porch. I made Star a bed out of old towels Grandma said I could use. I placed her on top of the towels and eventually she folded her long legs under her and sat staring at me, saying "Maa!" every now and then.

It didn't take long before Grandpa looked up from his computer and said, "It says here mother deer almost never abandon their babies. It says that unless you see the mother dead nearby, to leave the fawn where you found it and wait for the mother to come back."

I leaned over Grandpa's shoulder so I could see those words for myself. And I did. Unless you see the mother dead. And I allowed myself to think the thought that had been pushing its way up since I'd found her: What if her mother was the deer I had hit?

"I don't want to take her back," I said.

"We can't keep a wild animal in our house," said Grandma, poking her head through the open doorway.

"Can we just keep her for a couple of hours?"

"Her mother might be looking for her," said Grandma. "You should take her back now."

Blood pumped through my temples. I could feel myself on the verge of shouting at Grandma. I tried to remember what Dr. Shrink had taught me. Take deep breaths. Count to ten.

The article online had definitely said to leave the fawn alone. There was no point in trying to argue with Grandpa about that.

But what if Star's mother didn't come back?

I took a deep breath, and tried to keep my tone of voice level. "How about if I take her back now and then go back and check on her in a few hours, and if her mother hasn't come back, then bring her in?"

Grandpa and Grandma looked at each other.

"We'll cross that bridge when we come to it," Grandpa said. "Do you remember where you found her?"

I nodded. Glumly, I gathered Star back into my arms. Her little heart beat rapidly against my chest. "Maa! Maa!" she said, kicking her spindly legs.

"Do you want me to go with you?" Grandpa said.

"No, that's okay." I trudged up the driveway and back out onto the road. Every few steps Star said "Maa!" At one point she struggled so much I was afraid I was going to drop her. I walked back to the spot in the woods where I'd found her. There was a big pine with bark missing on its trunk that I remembered.

I looked around, as far as I could see through the tree trunks, to see if there was any sign of her mother. Nothing.

I found the patch of underbrush where I'd found her, and, taking a deep breath, I put her down. She wobbled on her skinny legs. "Maa!" she said.

How could I leave her?

I stood looking at her. She seemed so forlorn, just standing there. I felt like crying. But I had learned about wildlife, from the time the volunteer had warned me not to feed the wild horses at the Outer Banks. She should be left to wait for her mother.

If her mother came back.

With one last longing look at her, I turned and walked away. After a few steps, I heard movement behind me and turned back to look. She had started to follow me.

What should I do?

I ran a short distance away and then turned around again. She had stopped.

"Maa!" she said.

I swallowed the lump in my throat, turned away and headed toward the road, practically stumbling. When I reached the road, I turned back to look again. She was gone.

Back at Grandma and Grandpa's, I was near tears.

"What's going to happen to Star?" I said, lying face down on the couch. "What if she wanders out into the road?"

"You did the right thing, honey," Grandma said.

"Promise if I go back late this afternoon and she's still there, I can bring her back?"

Grandpa and Grandma exchanged glances. After a minute, Grandpa said, "Sure. If she's still there this afternoon, I guess that would mean her mother isn't coming back."

Suddenly there was an energetic knock at the door.

"Who could that be?" Grandma Roberts said.

Noah! "I'll get it!" I swiped the tears from my cheeks and raced over. When I opened the door, Noah was standing on the porch, leaning on a black Liquid Force wakeboard.

"Caramba!" he said. His thin face broke wide in a grin. His longish wavy blonde hair was pushed behind his ears, and the sun from the lake's surface glinted off the small silver hoop in his earlobe. His nose was peeling. He was wearing a pair of blue striped boardshorts and a Nike t-shirt. "Told you I'd show up," he said. "I'm always up for wakeboarding."

"Hey!" My heart kind of beat faster, but I acted very cool as I held the door open. "Come on in."

"Are you okay?" he asked.

"Yeah, sure, sure."

Picking up his board, Noah awkwardly stepped inside, looking around at my grandparents' small old-fashioned kitchen and the long oak dining table that Grandma Roberts liked to load with food and surround with family.

Grandma and Grandpa came into the kitchen.

"Hello, there," Grandpa said to Noah.

Noah leaned his board against the wall and quickly

stepped forward to shake Grandpa's hand politely. "Hello, sir, I'm Noah Edwards."

"Good to meet you." Grandpa looked at me quizzically.

"Hello," said Grandma Roberts, and Noah took her hand as though he was going to kiss it, but just bent over it slightly. Then released it.

"Nice to meet you, ma'am."

"You, too," she said, squinting at me thoughtfully. "Did Diana know you were coming, Noah?"

Noah laughed and scratched his head, mussing his hair. Then he pushed his hair behind his ear. "Uh ... I'm not sure." He raised his eyebrows and grinned at me. He was trying not to get me in trouble, so he was being as vague as possible.

"I invited him!" I said. "Sorry I didn't mention it. I figured it would be okay if we had another skier."

"Sure!" Grandpa spread his arms wide. "The more the merrier!"

"So, where's Stephanie?" Noah asked. "I thought she was staying here this weekend too."

"She was, but her mom came and got her last night. She changed her plans."

Noah nodded thoughtfully. "Oh. Bummer."

"Want to go down on the dock?"

"Sure."

"Let me just go put on my bathing suit." I ran

upstairs and, rushing to find my bathing suit, dumped my suitcase out on the bed. I wished Stephanie hadn't left. I could've asked her which bathing suit to wear or maybe even borrowed one of hers. I put on a black two-piece that she and Mom had talked me into getting. But then I was embarrassed and put a t-shirt over it. I skimmed back downstairs.

"I'll be down to drive the boat in a little while," Grandpa was saying. "Meanwhile, do you kids want to take the kayak out? There's an osprey nest out there by the island and babies may be in it."

"Want to?" I said to Noah.

"Sure!"

"The lifejackets and paddles are on the sun porch," Grandpa said. He loaded us down with them, and once Noah grabbed his wakeboard, we headed down the wooden walkway through the yard toward the dock.

"Guess what just happened?" I said. "I just found a baby fawn in the woods." I told Noah about finding Star, and Grandpa and Grandma making me take her back.

"I wish I could've seen it," Noah said. "My uncle hunts deer."

I cringed. "Ugh, don't even talk about it. How can it be fair? A guy with a gun against a beautiful living creature running for its life."

"He brings us venison sometimes."

"Ugh, stop!" I thought I was going to gag. Why was Noah saying this stuff? We were down by the water now, standing beside the bright orange two-seater kayak.

"I'm just sayin'!" Noah said, laughing. "Some people call deer rats with legs. They come in your yard and eat everything. They gobble up tulips and entire tomato plants."

I gave Noah a smack on the arm. "Quit it, right now! I love that little fawn I found."

"I'm just giving you a hard time," Noah teased, laughing. "I like to see you get mad."

"Oh, yeah?" I could feel myself blushing. "Why?"

"I don't know. Because you get so worked up about things, that's why."

I suddenly felt self-conscious and didn't know what else to say. I turned away and started putting on my life jacket.

"Hey, I'm kidding!" he said.

"Okay." Grabbing the handles on either end of the kayak, we carried it out onto the dock, and dropped it in the water.

"Do you want front or back?" I said.

"I'll take the back," he said. "I'd rather steer and let you do all the paddling work, ha ha."

"Very funny!" I said, but I grabbed one of the double-bladed paddles and lowered myself into the front seat.

Noah threw his t-shirt onto the dock, yelled "Cannonball!" and jumped over the kayak into the water, setting the kayak rocking and sending up a huge spray of water.

"Noah!" I yelled, grabbing the dock to steady the kayak.

He surfaced, laughing, and tossed the water from his hair with a jerk of his head. "Water feels great!" Then he pulled himself onto the kayak, streaming with water. He put on the other life vest, clicking the clasps shut, then pulled the paddle across his lap. "This is awesome," he said. "Perfect day."

"Okay, now, you have to stroke when I do otherwise our paddles will smack into each other." I took a stroke.

Noah took one a second later and smacked right into mine. "You mean like that?"

"Noah!"

We tried again, and our paddles clashed once more. We both started laughing. Then Noah paddled all on one side, and we started going in a circle.

"Noah!" I was laughing so hard. Then, with the end of his paddle, he pushed against my shoulder and I fell right in the lake, screaming.

"Oops!"

"I can't believe you did that!" I scrambled back up onto the kayak, while Noah laughed. My t-shirt was sticking to me and I was relieved I had on the lifejacket to cover it up. Finally I pointed to the small uninhabited island several hundred yards out of our cove into the main channel of the lake. We started paddling out there.

The sun beat down on us, flashing reflections from the water's smooth surface, and the prow of the kayak cut smoothly through the water. Since Noah was behind me, I couldn't see him. I tried to crane my neck around to see if he was stroking in the right coordination with me. In the cove, the water was calm, but as soon as we got into the main channel, the water became choppier. Small wavelets slapped the side of the kayak and rowing became harder.

"So, what made Stephanie decide to leave?" Noah asked.

"She wanted to be with her mom, I guess."

"Is she coming back?"

"Oh, I don't think so."

"So, it's just you and me, then."

Did I imagine it, or did he sound happy about that?

12

STEPHANIE

I know Mama was trying to make up for saying she was going to leave, because right after the first store we shopped in, she took me to another pricier one and didn't even make me go to the sales racks.

"These are cute shorts." She held up a pair of light colored distressed jeans shorts. "Why don't you try these?"

I took a white sleeveless dress with a wide black ribbon around the waist from the rack, and Mama nodded approvingly. "That would be really cute on you, sugar."

Normally, I loved shopping. I loved touching the fabrics, looking at their bright colors, and standing in the fitting room and seeing how I looked in an outfit. Having the perfect outfit helped me feel confident in school. Anywhere. I loved the pretty shopping bags, the way the salespeople neatly folded and stacked your purchases and wrapped tissue paper around them. I loved it when you could spray yourself with the sample colognes in places like Nordstrom. Mama called it "retail therapy."

Mama had come in the fitting room with me so she could see the outfits, and stood back against the wall, so when I looked at myself I could see her face just behind mine. We looked so much alike, with our dark hair and olive skin and ski jump noses. If I wanted to know what I was going to look like in thirty years all I had to do was look at Mama.

I wanted to tell her that she didn't have to buy me stuff. I still loved her no matter what. I wanted to tell her that I almost wished I wasn't there to complicate her life. I wished she could just go be with Barry and not worry about me.

I stared at myself in the white dress.

"It looks darling on you, sugar."

I turned sideways, then I fluffed the flounces on the skirt. Mama was planning on leaving tonight. Matt and I would be at the house together. Things were a little better but, still. Maybe I could get Colleen to invite me over to her house. If she was going to Hunter's party, I could just go with her, even if I wasn't invited.

"What do you think, sugar? Do you like it?"

"I think I got a text," I said. I got out my phone and, standing so Mama couldn't see the screen, I texted Colleen.

Can I spend the night at your house tonight? Can your parents come pick me up from Mama's?

I slipped my phone back into my purse, making sure the sound was on so I would see her answer right away.

"So?" Mama asked. "Who was it from?"

I didn't like lying to Mama. But I hadn't even gotten a text. And I didn't want Mama to know I was texting Colleen or why.

"Diana," I said.

"Oh! I didn't know you two had gotten close."

"Oh. Yeah, sort of."

"Really? Well, you have had to spend a fair amount of time together. I guess it would be bad if you didn't get along." Mama's phone dinged. She turned away from me to read it. And then she tapped in an answer, still turned away.

I took off the white dress and tried the shorts with

a pink tank that we had picked. My phone dinged and I grabbed it.

Sure. What time?

I'll text when I get back to Mama's.

As I put my phone away I had a funny thought: Mama and I were standing in a dressing room together, both hiding our texts from each other. I felt kind of bad, but maybe it wasn't so terrible. Nobody I knew had a completely honest relationship with her mother. It wouldn't be normal.

Mama bought me the dress as well as the tank and the shorts.

"Thanks, Mama." We walked back out into the mall, the shopping bag bumping gently against my leg.

"Oh, you're welcome, sugar. I love buying things for you." Mama wrapped her arm around my shoulders and squeezed, then glanced at her jeweled watch. "Well, we better head over and put our name in at the Cheesecake Factory. They always have a wait on Saturday night."

We strolled through the mall, me swinging my shopping bag, and who should be coming out of the Apple Store but Hunter Wendell and his friend Kerry Donovan.

"Hey!" Kerry, always totally wired, stopped and did a double-take at seeing me.

"Hey!" I laughed and switched the bag from one hand to another. Both guys had been in my Biology class last year. Kerry raised his hand a lot, and asked a bunch of questions everybody knew were to try to waste time and get the teacher off-track, while Hunter hardly said anything, but always made one of the highest grades in the class. I was sure he had absolutely no clue I had a crush on him.

"Hello there, boys," Mama said. She'd met them both at Friday night games. "Kerry and Hunter, right? What are you boys up to today?"

Kerry held up his laptop. "Had to get my laptop fixed."

"Oh, and did you get everything taken care of?"

"Yep."

"So, how are your summers going, boys?" Mama asked

"I'm looking for a job," Kerry said. "It's a drag. Most people don't want to hire fifteen-year-olds. Except they'll hire Hunter, he's so responsible." He poked Hunter, laughing. "I'm just a goof-off, nobody wants to hire me."

"I'm lifeguarding at Running Brook pool," Hunter said.

"Oh, great. So, how boring is that?" Mama said.

The boys laughed, and shuffled their feet around. Hunter had light brown hair and that kind of coloring where his cheeks turned a dusky pink when he blushed.

Kerry glanced at me, kind of smiling. He thought the whole situation was funny.

"I don't think it's boring," Hunter said in a serious tone. "When the little kids are in there, you've got to be alert."

"Yeah, I'm teaching tumbling to little kids and I feel like if I look away for even a few seconds they'll run off somewhere," I said, nodding in agreement.

Kerry touched my arm. "Hey, what are you up to tonight? Hunter's having a party."

"Oh, really?" I pretended I didn't know about it. My heart tripped as I looked over at Hunter.

"Yeah," Hunter said. "Here, put your number in my phone and I can text you the address and the time and everything." He handed me his phone, warm from his pocket.

"I'm not exactly sure what I'm doing tonight," I told him, trying to play it cool, as I tapped in my number. Hunter Wendell, getting my number! Inviting me to his party! I handed his phone back and I got goose bumps as my fingers touched his.

"I'm afraid Stephanie can't come," Mama said. "I have to go out of town and she's staying with her stepbrother. But would you boys like to join us at the

Cheesecake Factory for dinner? We were just heading that way."

I dropped my jaw. Mama was inviting them to dinner? What in the world had gotten into her? I was mortified.

Kerry and Hunter exchanged a wide-eyed look.

"Oh," Hunter glanced at his phone for the time. "We've got to get back to get ready for the party."

"Oh, okay," I said, relief flooding me. I wanted to hang out with Hunter, but not with Mama!

Thirty minutes later Mama and I were sitting in a booth at the Cheesecake Factory.

"Get anything you want," Mama said. "My treat!" She squeezed my arm. "Sugar, I'm so glad things are good between us again. I can't stand it when we argue."

"I don't like it either," I agreed.

"You don't mind that I'm going to meet Barry in Asheville tonight, do you? You understand. And you'll be fine with Matt for one night."

"Sure." I gave her a little smile. She had chosen me for one day, and I was grateful for that. Now she was choosing Barry. I had made a mistake to say it, though, and I had learned better than to do it again.

After lots of discussion with the server, Mama ordered a salmon salad. The server stood in his tight white apron, his pen poised above his pad, waiting for me to decide between the crab cake sandwich and the shrimp with angel hair. And then my phone dinged.

I peeked at it quickly.

Maybe ur plans will change and u'll be able to make it to the party tonight.

It was from Hunter.

13

DIANA

Noah and I paddled toward the osprey nest, just off-shore of the island. It was a manmade pole and basket, about twenty feet high, topped with a messy nest of sticks and pine boughs that the birds built. Standing on the top of the nest was the female osprey, regal and white with black wings and mask-like markings over her piercing eyes.

"Let's get closer and see if there are babies!" I said.

"Okay."

Our paddles were almost synchronized now, skimming

over the choppy surface of the lake, closing the distance between us and the osprey nest. The wind blew in our faces, and my shoulder muscles started to burn.

As we paddled closer, the female raised her white-tipped black wings in a threatening way and gave a haunting cry.

"Whoa, I don't think she likes us," Noah said.

"I just want to get close enough to see!" I gave my paddle blades three or four more good pulls.

Pretty soon we could see the dark little beaks and heads of the chicks bobbing just above the edge of the nest.

"Look! There they are!" I paddled even closer, craning my neck upwards.

The female got more and more agitated. Then, suddenly, from a tall pine on the island, in swooped the male osprey, calling loudly, his anvil-shaped wings curved as if to attack. He flew right at us, with fierce cries. Started to dive at us.

"Look out!" Noah yelled. "He's after us!"

The bird flew in a wide circle around the nest and then soared back in our direction, angling his body in a dive. Noah and I ducked as he flew within a few feet of our heads, still screeching. He passed close enough for us to feel the swish of the wind from his powerful wings.

"Come on, paddle backward!" In a scramble, we

reversed our paddling like crazy, and got the kayak turned around heading away from the nest and back toward the side of the island. After circling the nest again, the osprey flew back to his tree, grasping a gnarled gray limb with his talons and fluffing his feathers triumphantly. The female, still at the edge of the nest, stretched her beautiful black and white wings wide and flapped them several times.

We sped for the shore of the island, then grounded the kayak and clambered off, pulling it up onto the coarse sand on the island's shoreline.

"Whew, that bird was dive-bombing us!" Noah said, as I laid both of our paddles across the center of the kayak.

"Yeah, they're really protective of their babies. Grandpa says the osprey mate for life, just like geese." We took off our lifejackets, then sat on the sandy shore of the small island, letting the lake water lap at our toes and the sun beat down on our heads and sore shoulders. I started wondering why I'd worn the T-shirt. I took it off, squeezed the water out of it, and tossed it on the kayak. Then I felt immediately self-conscious about sitting there with him in my bathing suit.

"How long do osprey live?"

"I don't know. These same birds have been building their nest here for at least the past five years, since I've been coming here."

Behind us stood a cluster of pine and oak trees, some fallen. You could walk around this entire island in about five minutes. It was almost as long as a football field, but not as wide.

Noah's hair was still slicked back from when he had jumped in the water earlier. "A bunch of guys spent the night on one of these islands once," he said. "It was crazy."

"Yeah?"

"Somebody brought an iPod dock and you know how music travels over the water? We were playing all this unbelievably loud music and we had a case of beer. It was wild."

"Did anybody catch you?"

He shook his head. "We were afraid the lake patrol would come, but they never did. We lucked out." He stretched out on the sand. "Zillions of bugs, though."

Noah's bare chest had a patch of golden fuzz right in the center. I hadn't thought about us being alone on an island until just this minute. A tingle spread up the back of my neck into my hairline, and I shivered even though it was in the eighties out here.

Dr. Shrink and I had talked about a lot of situations but this was one we hadn't talked about. Did Noah think anything about us being alone on an island?

Should I say something about it? We'd hung out tons of times, but not like this.

"My guitar's in my car," he said suddenly, raising up on one elbow. "I can serenade you and your grandparents when we get back."

"Oh, cool! What songs have you learned?"

" 'Wish You Were Here' by Pink Floyd." He hummed the first four twanging notes of the opening, playing dramatic air guitar, and then sang the line about two lost souls in a fish bowl.

"Cool." I laughed.

He dug up a handful of the reddish, coarse sand and let it sift through his fingers. "And I learned 'Skinny Love' by watching an online video."

"Cool." *Was "cool" all I could say?* What a loser. I picked up one of the tiny black closed mussel shells that were scattered around, and tossed it into the shallow water at the edge.

One shell lay open on the sand, shaped like tiny black angel wings. Noah picked it up and dropped it onto my leg.

"Hey!" I found another shell. Dropped it into his belly button.

"Whoo!" He used his thumb and index finger to flip away the shell. Then he scooped up several more shells, jumped to his feet, and tossed them at me. Then, with a laugh, he started running.

"Okay! Watch out, buddy!"

I jumped up and raced after him, up the beach

toward a place where the waves had eroded the sand. The water gently washed against a muddy cliff about two feet high, and Noah had to zigzag, splashing, through the water. I laughed as I ran, completely out of breath.

Noah clambered up the muddy cliff and ran barefoot through the small wooded area to cross to the other side of the island, yelling "Ow! Ow! Ow!" as he stepped on sticks and pine cones. Then he ran across the beach and into the water on the other side, the silvery water splashing around him. He dove and swam, then turned around and grinned, treading water.

I chased him, breathless and laughing, running out into the water, diving at him, swimming in his direction. The minute I got close, he clapped his hands on my head dunking me.

Gasping and sputtering, I surfaced and tried to dunk him, but he pulled away with one strong stroke. "Ha-ha-ha!"

"I'll get you!"

Finally I lunged at him. I knew he was letting me catch him because I got my arms around his waist.

"Gotcha," I said, pulling tight and hugging him, my ear against his chest.

And for an instant, there was his heartbeat, solid and steady, in my ear.

Then his hands were around my waist and our arms

were around each other. I looked up and his face was inches from mine.

I closed my eyes. Held my breath. And then, like a bolt of electricity, like a wave breaking over our heads, his lips touched mine. They weren't soft, but firm and determined.

My heart was thundering. Blood roared inside my head. What was this? We were just friends!

I let go of him and scrambled away, pushing water between us.

"What was that?" I yelled.

He threw his arms in the air and let his palms splash on the water. "I have no clue!"

"I didn't do it!" I said.

"Neither did I!"

We stood in the waist-deep water glaring at each other. The sun had dropped toward the horizon and the shadows of the trees on the water were long. The wind had died and small ripples surrounded us, radiating outward on the smooth water.

"That was a mistake," I said.

"Definitely. A mistake."

"I need to check on Star."

On the ride back, we didn't talk. The only sounds were the wind at our backs and the dipping of the paddles and the slap of the waves against the kayak. I kept thinking about his lips when we touched. I'd thought lips would be soft and his weren't. Every time I thought about it I had this squiggly feeling deep in my stomach.

Back at the dock, the two geese greeted us. The female sat on the eggs on the boat cover and the male swam nearby, honking at us as we pulled the kayak up onto the dock.

"We're not going to hurt your wife or the eggs," I told him. "Just chill."

Noah and I kept our distance. We didn't talk. Thoughts raced through my mind and I replayed that kiss, with a shiver. What had it meant? As he grabbed his wakeboard and we headed up for the house, blood kept pounding in my ears.

"So? How was the kayak ride?" Grandpa Roberts held the door open for us.

"Fine," I mumbled.

"I have to get home," Noah said.

"Don't you want to wakeboard?" Grandpa asked.

"That's okay."

"So soon?" Grandma said from the kitchen. "I was just getting ready to invite you to dinner, Noah."

"He's got to go, Grandma," I said.

"Maybe tomorrow?" Grandpa looked from one of us to the other with a puzzled expression.

"I don't know. I better get going. Thanks anyway. Nice meeting you."

Grandma and Grandpa chorused back with "Nice to meet you," and "Come back."

Noah nestled his wakeboard under his arm, and I followed him out onto the porch.

I felt short of breath. I tried not to look at his lips. "Well. Bye."

"See ya." He held the wakeboard over his chest like a shield. "All right, so ... bye."

He trotted across the yard, climbed into his beat-up olive green Jeep and drove away.

I stood on the porch, watching the road long after he had disappeared. So, if he hadn't kissed me, and I hadn't kissed him, how had we kissed?

The shadows lengthened and the setting sun drizzled liquid gold on the water. As a cooler breeze threaded through the oaks in the back yard, the father goose swam back and forth, back and forth, guarding the nest. Birds chattered in the trees before sunset.

And suddenly I remembered. Star!

I yelled to Grandma and Grandpa through the screen. "I'm going to look for Star!"

I took off running, up to the road. I hiked down until I was even with the tree with the missing bark, then plunged into the dark shadowed woods. My footsteps made faint crunching sounds as I stepped on the pine needle ground cover, and I swiped dogwood branches, with their heart-shaped leaves, out of my way.

Noah's face flashed before me. The sound of his heart against my ear. I relived the kiss, then was glad there was no one in the woods to see me blush. Kissing didn't feel as innocent as I'd thought. Did I have stronger feelings for Noah than I'd admitted to before? Everything was such a surprise.

I stopped beside a bramble of underbrush and gave my head a shake, trying to refocus on Star. Was this where I had left her? I knelt and peered underneath the overhanging branches. Nothing.

I walked a large circle around the area, checking every other patch of underbrush. I wanted to talk to Stephanie about the kiss. I'd text her when I got back.

After wandering for fifteen minutes, I finally decided to give up. I would never see Star again. I should be happy for her. The fact she wasn't here meant her mother had come to get her. She was safe. It was good news.

I wandered back to the original spot. Once again knelt and crawled back to the far corner underneath.

And there she was. Lying as still as she could be, her large eyes staring at me.

"Star! You're still here!"

I don't know if the emotion of the afternoon was getting to me, but tears sprang to my eyes. Her mother hadn't come back for her. She was probably dead. And maybe it was because of me. More than ever, I felt responsible for Star. I had to save her. I'd killed her mother.

I reached inside the bush and gently wrapped my arms around her.

"Maa!" Her bleating was softer now. I most definitely needed to get her something to eat. I carried her back to the house. She didn't struggle as much as before. Her skinny legs hung down, bumping against my stomach. I ran up the porch steps, calling to Grandpa.

"She was still there!"

In only a few minutes, we had her back on her towel bed on the sun porch. Grandpa sat in a lawn chair with his laptop.

"Goat's milk. And baby bottles," he announced within a few minutes. "They have a four-chamber stomach and they have to suck on the bottle to open the second chamber. You can't let them lap from a dish. Unless it's water. So we can give her water."

I raced to the kitchen and brought back a plastic dish of water for Star. I set it down next to her.

"Where can we get goat's milk?" I asked.

"I believe they have it in the grocery store," said Grandma.

"Well, let me get my car keys," Grandpa said.

I jumped to my feet.

"Are you going to leave me here with that little thing?" Grandma asked.

"We won't be gone long, Grandma," I said, heading for the door.

"That little thing is going to poop on my sun porch," Grandma said, crossing her arms over her chest.

When we got back from the store, with three cartons of goat's milk and a set of two plastic baby bottles, Grandma met us at the door.

"That little thing is very insistent," she said. "It's definitely hungry. It's been crashing around bumping into the windows and making that bleating sound. It's finally laid down."

I began washing the baby bottles.

"Be sure to warm the milk," said Grandpa. "And it says about four ounces every three hours. You're going to be up all night."

"That's okay." I warmed a bottle with goat's milk in the microwave and shook it up, then headed out to the sun porch. Star was curled on her bed, but leaped to her feet bleating when she saw me.

Now, how to feed her. I knelt beside her and held the bottle up to her nose. Her nostrils flared as she sniffed and her eyes widened, but she didn't take the nipple into her mouth. I squeezed a little milk out onto my finger and rubbed it on her round black nose, but she tossed her head away. I tried to push the nipple into her mouth and she jerked her head.

"It says to hold the bottle high, so she has to turn her head up like she's nursing from her mother," Grandpa said.

I tried it. "Hmm. She's hungry, but she won't take the bottle."

"It seems as though she doesn't know what to do," Grandpa agreed.

I wrapped my arm around her neck and tried shoving the nipple into her mouth. She jerked her head away and then tried to run away from me, her long legs stumbling over ski vests and ski ropes. Then she came back and licked my arm, bleating again.

"Look how confused she is," I said.

Grandpa was on the computer again. "It says that sometimes they don't take to the bottle right away. Sometimes it's a struggle."

"No kidding." I wrapped my arm around her neck again and this time tried forcing the bottle into her mouth with both hands. She pulled her head out from under my arm and backed away, tripping over a pile of pillows. She made a funny sound like a kazoo.

"Once she figures out it's something to eat, she'll start to suck, don't you think?" I asked. Then I stood over her, practically sitting on her, and tried to shove the bottle into her mouth that way, so she couldn't back away. She turned her head and struggled to get away from me, kicking up a storm with her tiny hooves. She had gotten me on the shin once and it was throbbing and I was getting out of breath.

Star stumbled to the corner of the room, staring at me.

"Let her take a break for a little while," suggested Grandpa.

"How am I going to feed her if she keeps acting like this?"

"I don't know." Grandpa kept reading. "It says to move the bottle back and forth to imitate the way it nurses from its mother."

"If I can ever get her to take the bottle." I went and looked at the page Grandpa was reading. The fawn in the picture had its head turned up and it was drinking greedily from the bottle. I growled with frustration. Why couldn't I get Star to do that?

Grandpa and Grandma and I stood on the sun porch, with dusk setting in, watching Star, who had decided she didn't like the bed I'd made for her now, either, and had curled up almost inside a ski vest.

"That little thing has a mind of its own," Grandma said.

"It says sometimes it helps to stick your finger in the side of their mouth," Grandpa said, glancing up from the computer. "And then ease the nipple in."

Star stood up and began licking my arm. I tried again.

I cradled Star's head under my arm and held the bottle above her mouth. I squeezed a little milk out and let her sniff it. She licked my finger. I slid my finger into the side of her mouth, then took the opportunity to shove the bottle between her lips. She started to toss her head and then, somehow tasting the milk, she opened her big eyes wide. Eagerly, she grasped for the nipple of the bottle. I pushed the bottle farther into her mouth and the muscles in her throat began to contract as she began to drink. Now she was practically pulling the bottle out of my hand.

"She's drinking it! She's drinking it!"

Suddenly enthusiastic, Star scrambled to her feet. I stood and held the bottle above her head. I pushed and pulled, the way the articles Grandpa had read said to do.

Star was now making a racket, loud sucking sounds and panting while she tried to suck down the contents of the entire bottle in a few seconds.

"She seems like she's starving," Grandpa said.

"Just look at that little thing," Grandma said, sounding affectionate toward Star for the first time. "It was hungry."

Within a few seconds, the bottle was empty. She kept pulling on the empty bottle, gasping, with her eyes wide and enthused. She started licking my arm again.

"Do you think I should give her another one?"

Grandpa checked the laptop. "It just says four ounces every three hours. So I guess we ought to wait before feeding her again."

I knelt beside Star as she nuzzled my arm and the bottle. She was so cute I could barely stand it. "That's enough for now, little girl."

"Come on now, you two, I've been holding dinner for an hour now waiting for you to take care of that fawn," said Grandma. "Let's wash your hands and eat!"

I gave Star a quick pat on the head and went back through the living room to the kitchen. When I turned, I saw Star heading after me. "Can she come in the house, Grandma?"

"Absolutely not! She'll poop on my carpet. At least the floor of the sun porch can be cleaned."

Star, of course, paid no attention to what Grandma said and scampered right into the living room. She walked past the couch, looking curiously around, her little hooves sinking into the carpet. Then she plodded past the dining room table and onto the linoleum floor of the kitchen.

"She seems so funny walking around the house!"

"Back out on the porch, Diana!"

"Okay." I put the baby bottle into the sink and then

picked Star up and carried her back out to the porch. I settled her in her bed. A quiet, nagging thought kept repeating in the back of my mind.

Mom and Norm would be back tomorrow. I knew they weren't going to let me bring her home.

14

STEPHANIE

"You two are going to be all right?" Mama stood by the kitchen door with her overnight bag on her shoulder and her car keys dangling from one hand, looking at me, and then at Matt, who was sitting on a stool at the counter playing a game on his phone.

"Fine," I said. All my mixed feelings about everything had tangled up into a big old knot. Part of me didn't want to be any trouble to her, part of me felt so hurt, and part of me wanted her to leave so I could text Colleen and have her parents come get me.

"Matt, I'm counting on you," Mama said.

"At some point, you have to trust me," Matt said in a matter-of-fact voice.

"I wouldn't be leaving if I didn't," Mama said. "And I can always count on you, Stephanie."

I looked at the floor. Mama thought she could always count on me. Mama trusted me. Well, what about me being able to count on her?

"All right, then." Mama gave me a tight one-armed hug. "Be good, sugar." She looked like she was hesitating about whether to hug Matt, then decided against it. "I'll text when I get there."

And she shut the door. I leaned against the counter and listened to her car start and retreat up the driveway.

A flushed prickle of anger swept over me, then I immediately felt guilty for being mad. Mama had a right to be happy, and Barry made her happy. I glanced at Matt, still focused on his phone.

I was not going to be afraid of him. He was being nicer. Anyway, we were only going to be together for a few minutes. I knew he wouldn't tell on me. Not after all that he'd done.

I got out my phone. Now was the time. I texted Colleen.

Hunter invited me to the party. Can I get a ride?

I took a deep breath. I'd just gone behind Mama's back. But she'd left! While I waited for Colleen to answer, I saw that I had also gotten a picture text from Diana. I opened it and saw the sweetest little spotted fawn lying on Grandma and Grandpa's sun porch. A fawn! The message below said she'd found it, named it Star, and was feeding it from a bottle. Typical Diana. How could we do anything without Diana getting involved with some animal? I had to admit, I was curious.

"Hey," I said to Matt. "Diana found a fawn and is feeding it from a bottle."

"No way."

"Way," I said. "She found it in the woods."

Matt put down his phone to look at the picture. "Aww."

My phone dinged. Colleen.

Be there in 20. What r u wearing?

What *was* I wearing? I better go get changed. A tingle of excitement ran up my spine, thinking about seeing Hunter. I couldn't believe he'd invited me.

I went upstairs and put on the tank and jeans shorts that Mama had gotten me today. I looked at myself in the mirror over my dresser. Would people be wearing skirts at this party? Dresses? Should I wear the sundress instead?

Maybe I'd borrow some of Mama's perfume. I went down the hall and into her and Barry's room, hesitating just a minute outside the dark doorway. I used to go in Mama and Daddy's bedroom but I didn't go into Mama and Barry's. I turned on the light and went past the king-sized bed with the brocaded comforter into the powder room where she kept her perfumes, makeup, and jewelry box. I used to love watching her get dressed to go somewhere. She'd taken her favorite perfume with her, but an almost empty bottle of another stood on the granite bathroom countertop. Looking at myself in the mirror, I sprayed it on my wrists and behind my ears, just like I'd seen her do.

I could talk to Hunter about his lifeguarding job. In addition to swimming, he had also played soccer on the JV soccer squad this past year. He'd said in Biology that he wanted to be a doctor. I wondered if one or both of his parents were doctors. I'd probably meet them tonight. I'd seen them sitting in the stands at games and stuff like that but never met them.

How many people were going to be there? Would it be mostly sophomores? Colleen and I had been invited, but what other freshmen had?

I ran my palm over the smooth wood of Mama's jewelry box. I had always wanted to try on Mama's pearls. Now was my chance. They were cool to my touch as I lifted them from the small compartment where they were coiled, and felt smooth and heavy against my neck as I clasped them. They had a pinkish cast, and they seemed to glow softly. Mama told me real pearls feel cool at first but quickly absorb the warmth from your skin.

I looked at myself in the mirror. The pearls made me look more like Mama. All of a sudden I didn't want to look like her or be like her. In a rush, I unclasped the pearls. As I was putting them back, my phone dinged.

On our way!

From Colleen. I ran my brush through my hair once more, slicked on some lip gloss, and headed downstairs.

"Is there such a word as *shamt*?" Matt asked as I entered the kitchen.

"I don't think so. You could take off the *t* and have *sham*," I said.

"I need that triple word space."

"Oh. Well, what other letters have you got? You could do *mash* and add an *ed* to it or something."

"Hmm." He looked up from his game and saw my outfit. "You going somewhere?"

"Oh, yeah. I got invited to a party, and my friend Colleen's parents are giving me a ride. I'll be back later."

"Does your mom know you're going?"

"No." I played nervously with the zipper on my

purse. "But I'll just be gone for a few hours. Anyway, she probably doesn't care."

Matt tilted his head at me. "What makes you say that?"

I shrugged. I wasn't used to having one-on-one conversations with Matt. He wasn't exactly someone I felt like opening up to.

When I didn't answer, he put down his phone and looked at me earnestly. "One thing I found out when I had my accident was how much my parents *do* care. I mean, Dad and Mom both went without sleep for the first few days waiting for me to wake up. And I saw both of them like, lose control and break down crying. It made me think twice. I realized that they probably care about me more than anything else."

I nodded. "Yeah, Barry scared me speeding to the hospital."

"Seriously. So think about that. I'm not going to tell that you're going to this party or whatever, but don't make the mistake of thinking that your parents don't care. And, you know, don't drink and drive." He grinned and wagged his finger at me.

I laughed. A question that I'd wondered about came into my mind. "Since you were almost killed, do you ever think that maybe God saved you?"

Matt squinted at me. "What do you mean? I don't know, I don't think about stuff like that. Those sayings about God caring for every little bird — I don't believe that. Why would God care about me?"

"Why wouldn't he?" I asked. There seemed like so much more to say. I wanted to tell him that I thought he was wrong.

But just then my phone dinged. Colleen.

We're here.

I looked up at Matt. "Seriously, you should think about it. My ride's here. I'll be back later."

"Okay. Have fun."

Dusk was falling as I ran out to the driveway and jumped into the backseat with Colleen.

"Mm, you smell good," she said.

"Oh, no, did I put on too much?"

"Maybe a little."

How embarrassing! I tried rubbing the perfume off my wrists onto my shorts.

Fifteen minutes later, Colleen and I stood on the front step of a two-story colonial with a rose bush blooming beside the door. A deep pounding beat came from music inside and made the whole house vibrate. We waved goodbye to Colleen's parents, who were off to dinner and a movie before they returned for us. On the drive over, Colleen's mom asked if Hunter's parents were home, and Colleen answered, "Hunter's a straight A student. He would never have a party without his parents knowing about it."

But now, as her parents pulled away, she turned to me, put her long, straight blonde hair behind one ear, and said to me, "His parents are out and won't be home until later. They told him it was okay to have a few friends over."

My breath caught in my throat. The party was going to be totally different than I had expected. *Should I stay?* I immediately thought, but then I got mad at myself. *Of course I'm staying.* It would be okay. His parents had said it was okay for a few friends to come over. And Mama was on her way to Asheville. And Daddy and Lynn were out of town, having heart-to-heart talks with *Jon* and *Olivia*. I took a deep breath.

"No one's going to hear if we ring the doorbell," Colleen said. We pushed the door and it swung open. The front hall and living room, with shiny hardwoods and oriental rugs, were empty of people. Music blasted from the back of the house.

"Come on." Colleen pushed me over the threshold.

A guy and a girl I didn't know stood just outside the kitchen entrance with their arms wrapped around each other. The girl was whispering in the boy's ear. Colleen and I edged past them and stepped into the kitchen.

Four people were sitting around the kitchen table playing Spoons. As we walked in, someone grabbed a spoon, and chairs got turned over as everyone else lunged for the rest of the spoons in the center of the table. Jenna Wentworth and Carrie Shepherd, two girls from the JV soccer team, each had one end of the last spoon and were yelling at each other.

"I got it!" Carrie shrieked, half laughing.

"Oh no you don't!" Jenna cried. She leaned back and pulled it from Carrie's hand until the spoon bent and slid from Carrie's hand. Jenna held the spoon over her head. "Yes!"

Carrie slumped back in her chair with a snort of disgust. "I hate this game!"

A second later, she sat up and pounded her fist on the table. "Rematch. Deal the cards."

On the counter, along with a couple of empty chip bags, a bowl that had once had some kind of light-colored dip in it had been scraped clean.

A couple of guys from the swim team sat on the sofas in the sun room, one with a guitar. The sliding door to the back deck was open and a bunch of JV soccer players sat around outside laughing and joking.

One of the swimmers looked over at us.

All of a sudden I felt like I was walking onstage

wearing a bathing suit with a spotlight on me. I wanted to die.

I put my hand on Colleen's arm, to steady myself. "I don't see Hunter anywhere. Do you know if any other JV cheerleaders were coming?"

"Beth and Ashley said they might."

"Where are they?"

We peeked out on the back porch, where everyone was talking about a summer soccer camp on a college campus. No Hunter.

"Hey," Colleen boldly asked one of the guys. "Is Hunter here?"

They all laughed.

"You would think so, since it's his house," one of the guys said. "Try the basement."

"Come out here and talk to us!" one guy yelled. "We won't bite!"

"Maybe later," Colleen said, laughing.

We headed back through the kitchen. "When I saw Hunter today at the mall, he was with Kerry Donovan," I said. "Look for Kerry."

We threaded our way to the basement stairs, through people watching the Spoons game, and started to make our way down. Music wafted up the stairs, along with the smack of billiard balls, the sharp rhythmic rap of ping pong balls, and the buzz of people talking and laughing.

As we went down the stairs, the air got cooler. I felt chilly in my tank and shorts, and shivered. But maybe that was because I was nervous.

Downstairs, I finally saw Hunter. He and Kerry were playing pool with a girl named Megan, who was also on the girls' soccer team. I had played some pool, since Mama and Barry had a pool table in the basement. It looked like they were playing rotation, where you start by trying to get the one ball in the pocket, and then the two, and so on, all the way up to fifteen. A few other people stood around watching. Two people were lying together on the couch beside the pool table kissing. The guy was rubbing his hand up and down the girl's back.

On the other side of the rec room, a guy and a girl were playing a wicked game of ping pong.

"Stephanie! Colleen!" Kerry yelled. "You made it!"

Everyone looked at us, and I felt heat rising to my face. I was afraid to look at Hunter.

Suddenly Kerry, using his pool cue like a microphone, started singing along with the song, about being glad we came. Everyone started laughing, and then Hunter picked up another cue and started singing along too, like they were in a boy band.

"... and make you glad you came!" they sang together, swaying beside the pool table, then they counted down and did a turn together. Everybody clapped, laughing.

I was laughing too, and I felt warm all over.

"Come play some pool," Hunter said. "We'll take you on after this game."

"Okay, sure!" Colleen said.

"Okay." I smiled shyly at Hunter. He was dressed very preppie, with khaki shorts and a polo shirt.

"Have a Coke or something," Kerry said, pointing to a refrigerator behind a bar in the corner.

"You act like you live here!" Colleen joked.

"He practically does," Hunter said.

The chorus to "Glad You Came" blasted through the basement again and Kerry and Hunter sang into their pool stick microphones and turned around, laughing.

I took a deep breath.

15

DIANA

The microwave dinged and I opened it, and reached for the bottle. Shaking to mix it, I headed through the family room, past Grandma and Grandpa Roberts on the couch watching a *Masterpiece Classic* they had taped.

"Time for your bottle!" I told Star as I pushed open the sliding door to the sun porch. Star, lying on a pile of ski vests, scrambled to her feet.

"Maa!" she said. She had become attached to me

already. When I was on the sun porch she followed me like a dog.

I knelt beside her and draped one arm over her neck, held the bottle up, and she eagerly grasped the nipple and began drinking. I made the push-pull motion that had been described in the online article.

"Yum, is that good?" I talked to her softly while I held her warm little body close to mine. She sure was noisy! She made loud sucking and breathing noises as she drank. But I liked hearing it. I was keeping her alive.

But what was going to happen tomorrow? Mom and Norm would never let me take her home. We didn't have a sun porch at home. Where would I keep her ... my room? What was I going to do with her?

The article had said that fawns should be fed only goat's milk for the first week, and then the second week grasses and grain should be added. The baby should be weaned by about eight weeks of age. I imagined myself feeding Star grasses and grains. I imagined her scampering around our back yard. I imagined myself keeping her in my bedroom for six weeks, or until she might be old enough to be weaned.

After she finished her bottle, she nudged me and said "Maa!" and stamped her little feet for more, but the article had said four ounces was enough. Eventually she curled up with her head in my lap, and I sat there, blissfully stroking her narrow head.

"Diana," Grandma said, standing in the doorway. She looked at Star with sadness in her eyes. I knew what she was about to say.

"Don't tell me, I don't want to hear it!" I said it so loudly Star scrambled to her feet and darted away from me. "Without me she would starve to death! I'm not going to let her starve!"

"Calm down, Diana," Grandpa said, coming to the door. "Grandma's right. We have to figure out what to do."

"I'm going to ask Mom if I can keep her," I said stubbornly. I got out my phone and thought about sending a text, then decided I might be better able to talk her into it if I called. I hadn't wanted to interrupt their weekend, but this was important. Grandma and Grandpa left the doorway, with doubtful looks on their faces.

"Diana, is everything okay?" Mom's voice sounded alarmed.

"Oh, yeah, everything's okay," I said. "How's your vacation going?"

"Fine." Now Mom's voice sounded suspicious. She wasn't going to talk to me about the marriage counseling, that was pretty obvious. "Has something happened?"

"Well," I said. And I told her about everything, from

hitting the deer to finding Star. I told her I'd taken Star back once, but that the mother had not come back for her. Surely Mom would understand how much I needed to keep Star. "I mean, I know I can't keep her forever. But what if I keep her until she's weaned, just a few weeks?"

"We have nowhere we could keep a fawn, Diana. You know that. Is there some expert you can call, someone who specializes in caring for orphaned wildlife?"

"I'm keeping her!" I yelled. "You can't stop me!"

Mom's voice warmed and became more gentle. "Diana. Remember what you learned about the wild horses? Wild animals are not meant to be kept as pets."

"Please!" I begged.

I counted. Mom was talking, saying something else about the well-being of the animals. My heart sank. I did remember what I had learned about the wild horses. I sat stroking Star's head. I ran my fingertips over her pear-shaped ears, her knobby forehead. I touched her amazingly long eyelashes. Yes, I remembered. My throat started to ache. My eyes to sting.

Part of it was just hearing Mom's voice. Every word she said, I strained to listen, trying to figure out how she sounded. If things were good.

"Do you want me to talk to Grandpa Roberts?" Mom said.

"No, that's okay." My voice came out flat. Moronic Mood-o-Meter at about two.

"I'm so sorry, honey. I know how attached you get to these animals. How are you and Stephanie getting along with Grandpa and Grandma?" Mom asked.

"Stephanie's not here."

"What?" Mom's voice rose in alarm. "What do you mean?"

So then I told her all about Stephanie's mom coming to get her. Mom seemed much more upset about this than she was about Star.

"Let me talk to Grandma or Grandpa," she insisted. So I gave Grandma my phone, and she went into the kitchen.

While Grandma was talking to Mom, I took Grandpa's laptop out onto the sun porch with Star and looked up some more articles on caring for fawns. That's when I saw it. The paragraph about the wildlife rehabilitator.

"If you find an orphaned fawn, please contact a nearby licensed wildlife rehabilitator for help."

I looked up "licensed wildlife rehabilitator," and typed in Grandma and Grandpa's zip code. And a name and number came up. Kirsten Wiggins.

I sat with Star in my lap for several long minutes, staring at that name. Finally Grandma brought me back my phone.

"I think I might have found someone to call," I said. "About the fawn."

"Is that so?" Grandma said. Her footsteps were quiet as she came and laid her hand on the top of my head. "That sounds good, honey."

"I guess I'll do it now." I pulled Star's bony little body close to mine, where she curled next to my ribs and began grooming herself like a cat, carefully licking her own coat. Outside, the sun had set and crickets had begun to chirp. The water was dark as ink, with an indigo sky above. I took a deep breath. After a slight hesitation, I tapped in the number.

When I heard the voice that answered, I almost cried. I realized I'd been hoping no one would pick up.

"I found a fawn," I said. I pushed the tears away and kept on talking.

"Did you feed the fawn anything?" she asked, after I described finding Star. Her voice sounded so concerned and caring.

"I've given her two bottles of goat's milk," I said. "It was hard to get her to take the bottle but she finally did. Now she loves it and she makes a ton of noise!"

"Okay. Good," said Kirsten. "You've done a good job. Where are you located?"

"On Lake Norman." My heart was sinking as I described nearby landmarks, and gave the address.

"I have another person who has called me, and I

have to go there tomorrow morning, so I think I can get to you by mid-afternoon. Until then, keep giving the goat's milk about every three or four hours. I'll bring a dog crate for her."

"So you're going to take her?" My heart started beating funny. Star's ears twitched in my direction. She wobbled over and pressed her little black nose up to the window, leaving a smeary spot.

"Yes," said Kirsten. "That's my job. I'll bring her here to my house and I'll take care of her until she's ready to be released to the wild."

I swallowed. "Okay."

"I'll call you tomorrow when I'm on my way. Thank you for calling me. You've done the right thing."

After we hung up, I took Star out in the back yard so she wouldn't poop on the sun porch. I put an old piece of ski rope around her neck like a dog leash. Standing out there with her, I watched the moonlight dance on the water. I wanted to text Noah about all of this. I had gotten used to telling him what was going on with me. But after what had happened this afternoon I didn't know what to say to him. I closed my eyes and remembered the feel of his firm lips against mine. The way I couldn't catch my breath. The flip-flop deep in my stomach.

I opened my eyes, shook my head just to clear it. Did that mean we liked each other? It couldn't! Noah and I were just friends! What had happened was an accident!

And since I hadn't heard from him, I was willing to bet that he was probably thinking the same thing I was thinking. Thank God it was summer. Thank God I didn't have to see him in school next week. Still, I wished I could talk to him about Star.

Well, there was one person I could always talk to. Stephanie.

I took Star back inside, and she wobbled around the perimeter of the sun porch, testing how far she could go in each direction.

I got out my phone and texted Stephanie.

> Someone is coming to get Star tomorrow.
> I'm sad.

But, for the first time, Stephanie didn't answer my text.

16

STEPHANIE

"Let's play eight-ball," Hunter said.

"Fine, rack 'em up, fine sir," Kerry said, pointing his pool cue at Hunter with a flourish.

After Hunter and I beat Colleen and Kerry in our first game, Colleen and Kerry went upstairs. The guy and girl who had been pounding the ping pong ball across the net at each other threw down their paddles and went upstairs, too. Even the couple that had been making out on the couch left, leaving us downstairs alone. We kept playing eight-ball, and I could feel

Hunter's eyes on me every time I leaned over the table to reach a shot. Someone started playing a song about twenty-seven tattoos upstairs, and between shots we started dancing and singing along.

A tingle of excitement ran up my spine. Hunter was paying attention to me, only me. I'd surprised him by being able to play pool.

I took a shot, and my cue ball barely touched the number four ball, nudging it a few inches.

"It kissed the four," Hunter said, using pool lingo, but he smiled at me when he said it, and I could feel myself turning red. We were halfway through another game of eight ball when Colleen appeared on the stairs. "My parents are here," she said. "Time to go."

I leaned on my pool cue. I was stripes and Hunter was solids, and we each had two balls left on the table.

"Hang around," Hunter said. "I can give you a ride home."

"You could?" I knew I should go home with Colleen's parents, but Hunter and I had been joking around, and everything felt magical.

"Are you coming?" Colleen said. "You have to decide now."

I glanced at Hunter, who was chalking the end of his cue stick. His pastel polo shirt, his khakis, his pink cheeks.

Daddy would want me to go home with Colleen's

parents. Daddy wouldn't have let me come to this party in the first place. What would Mama want? I didn't know. She was so wrapped up in Barry, she probably didn't care.

"You sure you can take me home?" I asked Hunter.

"Yeah, no problem."

"Okay, then," Colleen said, and she snuck me a wink. "I'll tell my parents you have permission to stay, and I'll text you later." I watched her feet disappear as she headed up the stairs. "I hope you don't get in trouble," she called back.

Me too. Suddenly I felt nervous.

Hunter took a shot at the four in a corner pocket and just missed. The cue ball rolled to a stop lined up to put the eleven into another corner. Carefully, I leaned over the table and lined up my shot. Feeling Hunter's eyes on me, I leaned forward a little more. Gently, I hit the cue. The eleven dropped in.

"Where'd you learn to play pool?" Hunter asked as I circled the table, looking for another shot. Apparently I hadn't learned how to play well enough to line up my next shot like I'd seen Barry do.

"My stepfather has a table. When I was living with him and my mom, they used to play, and I'd play with them. I'm not very good."

"You're better than a lot of girls."

"Well, thanks." I rolled my eyes. "I think."

On his next turn, Hunter sank both of his solids but then missed the eight. He would win on the next turn if I didn't sink the nine now. I danced to the song playing upstairs, moving my hips, feeling like I had special powers, drawing Hunters's eyes to me. I made the angle too sharp and missed, leaving Hunter an easy angle on the eight.

"Too bad!" Hunter said. He put the eight in, winning the game.

"Shoot! I gave you that. Well, good game." I put my cue back in the rack on the wall, and headed for the stairs, thinking we'd go up now.

"Where're you going? Let's hang down here for awhile." He sat on the couch.

I hesitated. "Don't you want to see what's going on upstairs? People might be wrecking your house."

"I'm not worried." He patted the couch next to him. "Come on."

After a few seconds, I sat down next to him. Did he know I had a crush on him? Did I want to kiss him? My heart was skittering and my mouth felt dry. My thigh was touching his, and my skin tingled in that spot. What should I talk about? Diana seemed to think I was so good at this, but suddenly I was drawing a blank.

"So, have you ever had to save anybody while lifeguarding?" I finally asked him.

"Yeah, the first weekend I was lifeguarding was

Memorial Day, and the pool was really crowded. This little kid in the shallow end walked too deep and his face went under. His mom was talking to another mom and wasn't paying attention. I jumped in and scooped him up. It happened in like, a heartbeat."

"Whoa, scary. Good that you had your eyes on him."

"Yeah. It was kind of freaky since it was my first weekend. But nothing else has happened since then. Lifeguarding is weird because it seems boring just sitting there but, I mean, something could happen in the blink of an eye."

"Yeah. Do you have groupies?" I laughed as I said it. "When we used to go to the pool in our development, when we were about ten, we thought the lifeguards were really cool. We'd talk to them all the time."

Hunter laughed and his cheeks flushed pink. "Yeah, there's a group of ten year old girls who flirt with me all the time."

"Ha, I bet you love it."

Hunter gave a dismissive gesture.

Suddenly it sounded like a herd of elephants had stormed the house, as four guys from the swim team, juniors and seniors, pounded down the stairs.

"Hey, Wendell!" said one of the guys. "You didn't think you could have a party without inviting your old buddy Tyler, did you?"

Hunter stood up laughing, his face turning pink.

"Hey, how did y'all find out I was having people over? My parents just said I could have a few people."

"Word travels, my man. Word travels," Tyler said. He was carrying a tray with rows of tiny paper cups filled with what looked like green Jell-O. "And we all know no party is complete without . . ."

"Jell-O shots!" chorused the guys. Tyler put the tray down on the bar, and each of the upperclassmen took one of the small paper cups and downed the contents.

Hunter was laughing, but it seemed like he was embarrassed.

Tyler picked up a paper cup and held it out to Hunter with great ceremony.

"For you, my host with the most."

Hunter hesitated.

Tyler leaned close to Hunter. "Who's been your big brother on the team this whole year?"

"You have," said Hunter.

"Who took you under my wing and showed you the ropes?"

"You did."

"Who's had your back?"

"You have."

"Nothing matters when you're on the block except one thing. And what's that one thing?"

"Winning," said Hunter.

"That's right. Have a shot."

Hunter took one of the cups from Tyler and downed its contents.

"All right!" yelled all the guys.

Hunter kind of laughed.

"And who is this lovely young lady that you appear to be conversing with?" asked Tyler.

"Just a friend of mine. Stephanie."

For some reason I wished Hunter hadn't told them my name.

"Have a Jell-O shot, Stephanie," said Tyler. "Allow me." He picked one up and held it out to me as if he were someone's butler, and I was an aristocratic lady.

"Uh, no, thanks," I said, and kind of giggled, but my chest started to feel tight.

"Oh, come on. Look how small they are. Teeny tiny. Not a big deal at all."

"That's okay," I said. My face felt hot.

"She doesn't want one," Hunter said.

"I made these myself," said Tyler, with mock huffiness. "Are you going to insult me by refusing to even try one?"

Hunter started laughing. "Cut it out!" he told Tyler. "Stephanie, you don't have to have one."

"If she doesn't have one, then you need to have another one," said Tyler.

Hunter glared at him, then broke out laughing again.

"One more." All the guys cheered and Tyler clapped him on the back.

What was Hunter doing?

"Hunter," I said. "Weren't you going to drive me home?"

"He can still drive," Tyler said quickly. "He only had two."

"Yeah, no problem," Hunter said.

I didn't know what to do. I realized that since Colleen had left I really didn't know anyone else here other than Hunter. I knew the names of the girls on the JV soccer team, but they didn't know me. How could I have let this happen?

Hunter and the other guys from the swim team had now all put on goggles and were singing some song together from *Finding Nemo* that they always sang before a meet. I went out the sliding door to the outdoor patio, where there was a hammock hanging from the porch above. I crawled into the hammock.

Hunter had been so nice to talk to. Then those guys showed up and he was trying to impress them, and he totally changed.

Why had I stayed?

And then Daddy's ringtone started up on my phone.

I couldn't pick up. I couldn't tell Daddy where I was. I couldn't tell him I'd come to a party without permission and didn't have a ride home. He was up in the mountains with Jon and Olivia anyway, what could he do? I let voicemail take the call

Somehow I had to get out of here.

My mind raced. I couldn't ask Colleen's parents to come back for me. I couldn't call Matt. He'd lost his license. There was only one person I could call.

17

DIANA

When the text came, I was already in bed. I thought it might be Noah and grabbed my phone. But it was Stephanie.

Help! I'm at a party and I need a ride home!

What had happened? Wasn't Stephanie with her mom?

Where r you? R you ok?

Yes, I'm ok. Party with no parents.

She texted me an address. I recognized the neighborhood. Nice. In Charlotte. People from our school lived there.

I sat up in bed. My heart pounded and there was a buzzing in my head. What should I do? It would take forty-five minutes to get there from here. Grandpa and Grandma were asleep. I could wake them up, and ask Grandpa to drive. But I had no idea what might be going on with Stephanie. I didn't want to get her in trouble. I'd just go get Stephanie and take her to her mom's house. Grandpa and Grandma would never know.

Grandpa kept his car keys on a hook by the refrigerator. I'd sworn I'd never drive again after hitting that deer yesterday. But Stephanie needed my help.

B there soon.

I jumped into my jeans and a T-shirt, slid my feet into flip-flops, grabbed my phone and purse, and tiptoed down the stairs. Slowly, I took Grandpa's keys off the hook, freezing each time they clinked. I was barely letting myself breathe.

I glanced onto the sun porch, where Star was curled asleep, but didn't walk over. I didn't want to wake her up. I'd be back in time for her next feeding in a few hours.

Very slowly, I unlocked the side door that led outside to the driveway. It made a distinct "click" sound and I froze. I waited several seconds. No sounds from Grandpa and Grandma's room. Blood roared in my head.

I turned the doorknob and eased the door open. It made a sucking sound and I froze again. Still silence. I slipped out, gently pulling the door shut. The cool night air enveloped me.

What had happened to Stephanie? Would she be all right until I could get there?

Crickets sang and the stars spread over me. They were always more brilliant up here at the lake. A summer breeze rustled through the pine trees near the house, and in the back yard, the lake seemed to hum. I took silent footsteps, muffled by pine needles, out to the driveway. The car lock made a "thunk" sound as I unlocked it.

As quietly as I could, I opened the door and climbed in. With shaking hands, I adjusted the seat and fit the keys into the ignition.

Would it wake Grandpa and Grandma when I started the engine?

I took a deep breath and turned the key.

The engine roared. It seemed horribly loud over the cricket sounds. I waited to see if the house lights came on. But they didn't. Slowly, I backed out of the driveway and drove a short way down the road, glancing back at the house. Still no lights. Maybe Grandpa and Grandma were a little deaf. I turned on the headlights. Now. Just keep driving.

What would Grandma and Grandpa do if they woke up and found me and their car gone? Maybe I should've left a note. Too late now.

When I passed the place where I had hit the deer, I broke into a cold sweat. My headlights swept past the groves of pine and oak, and shone on the heart-shaped leaves of the dogwoods. I took deep breaths and concentrated on staying in the lane.

My hands were gripping the steering wheel so tightly they ached. I pulled to the side of the road and counted to ten, taking deep breaths.

Then I programmed the address Stephanie had given me into my phone's GPS.

Without seeing any other cars, I followed the narrow winding roads by the lake and soon I'd made it to the highway. I'd only driven on it a few times. I merged, the way Mom had shown me, and in seconds was headed down the interstate toward Charlotte.

It was past midnight, and the traffic was light. I stayed in the right lane, trying to keep my breathing steady as Dr. Shrink had taught me.

My senses seemed heightened. I felt hyperaware of everything. Everything, from car headlights to the lighted bridges to the gleaming stretches of water beside the highway, seemed crystal clear and sharp tonight. The moon floated behind a wispy gray bank of clouds.

Grandpa never turned on the air conditioning and I didn't want to try to figure out how to do it while driving so I felt around on the door until I found the button to crack the windows. Warm summer wind flowed in, making a loud flapping noise.

Suddenly my phone dinged. A text message. Maybe it was an update from Stephanie. I got off the next exit. Pulled onto an access road to check it.

R you on the way? Is Grandpa mad?

I texted back:

It's just me.

What??

I breathed in sharply. She expected me to tell Grandpa. Too late now.

B there soon.

I pulled onto the highway.

Not long afterward, a white car came up on my left side. I stayed steady in the right lane. As the car pulled alongside, I saw writing on the door. A cop!

My heart lurched. I kept my foot steady on the accelerator and my hands at ten and two on the steering wheel. Looked straight ahead. What if he pulled me over? But what could he pull me over for? Stealing a car? Had Grandpa woken up, seen the car gone, and called the police?

I took deep painful breaths. My knuckles were white on the steering wheel. My underarms were wet. Finally, after gliding along beside me for a few agonizing seconds, he passed on by. My heart thudded with relief.

What was happening with Stephanie by now? What kind of trouble was she in? Had she been drinking? Tried some kind of drug? Had a guy attacked her? All of those things seemed crazy, like stuff that would never happen to Stephanie. But normally Stephanie wouldn't even go to a party without parents. It might be something I'd do, without thinking, but not Stephanie. Why had she?

At last I got off the highway onto the major road near our house. Now I was in familiar territory and relaxed my hands on the wheel. I'd driven around here with Mom a lot. I drove past the school, and the neighborhood where Noah lived. The GPS showed that I should turn in at the stone and brick entrance to a nice neighborhood of mostly brick colonials that I'd been in a couple of times before.

I turned in. Pulled over to send Stephanie a text.

In the neighborhood. Come outside?

She answered right away.

Already am.

I wove my way down to a cul-de-sac lined with parked cars. At the end, Stephanie sat on the curb beside the mailbox, wearing a tank and jean shorts that I hadn't seen before. A rosebush bloomed just behind her, and loud music floated out from the house. Some dark figures stood on the front porch. She jumped to her feet and ran over to the car. She yanked the door open. Collapsed into the seat.

"Oh, thank God you're here!" She slammed the door, and then leaned over and hugged me, her long dark hair enveloping me. I could smell her perfume. "Oh, Diana, thank you, thank you! You were the only person I could call!"

A warm feeling spread through me. I was the only person!

She waved at me to drive. "Go, go, let's get out of here!"

I pulled quickly out of the cul-de-sac. Headed back through the neighborhood.

Stephanie struggled to put on her seatbelt, leaning back against the seat with a loud sigh. I glanced over and a streetlight caught shiny tracks of tears on her cheeks.

"Everything's gonna be okay."

"O-okay." She sniffled.

I turned back onto the main road. "So, how did you end up at this party anyway?"

"Hunter invited me this afternoon at the mall. I didn't know when he invited me that his parents weren't going to be back until later."

"Who's Hunter?"

"Hunter Wendell, in my Biology class. He's a sophomore." Her voice sounded small and so dejected. "I had a crush on him. And he said he could give me a ride home. So I stayed."

"So, what happened? Did he attack you or something?"

Stephanie took a breath. I pulled into a church parking lot. Looked at her closely. My headlights shone on a stained glass window. "What? What happened, Stephanie?"

"No-nothing, really. I'm just really glad to be out of there. I'm so glad you came and got me."

"You've got to tell me! What happened?"

"I don't know, we were downstairs playing pool, and these friends of his came and he started taking Jell-O shots. And I knew he couldn't drive me home. I mean, he's a nice guy. He makes good grades, and everything. It was just, he said he'd bring me home, and then he started drinking the Jell-O shots. I feel terrible. I was so stupid."

"Hey, it's not your fault! Did anything else happen?"

She shook her head vehemently. "No, no."

"Do you swear?"

She nodded, sniffling. "I just went outside and called you, that's all. He's still back there with his friends. He probably hates me now for leaving."

"Who cares how he feels about you, Stephanie? He's a jerk for doing that." I leaned over and hugged her again. I smoothed her hair and patted her back the way I liked for Mom to do for me. Stephanie had comforted me before. Was I actually comforting her?

She drew a ragged breath and wiped her palms across her face. "I shouldn't care, you're right."

She looked limp and defeated in the seat next to me.

"Easier said than done," I said, and sighed heavily and put the car in gear. "Okay, we better get going. I should take you back to your Mom's house, right?"

Stephanie's eyes went wide. "No! Mama's not there; it's only Matt. I don't want to go back there."

"But if I take you back to Grandma and Grandpa's, they'll find out I took the car."

"I don't want to go back to Mama's."

We stared at each other. I felt out of breath. "Well, back to the lake then. We'll just have to explain to Grandma and Grandpa. They'll have to understand that I had to come get you." I pulled out of the parking lot and headed for the interstate. I hadn't had a chance to ask her about what had happened to her mom. After only a mile or so, though, the car started acting funny. It started choking and cutting off.

"Oh, my gosh, what's wrong with the car?"

"I don't know!" The car was slowing down and wouldn't speed up even when I pressed harder on the accelerator. Panicked, I pulled over to the side of the road. It drifted to a stop.

"What's wrong?"

"I told you, I don't know!" I looked at the dashboard to see if there were any red warning lights on. And then I saw it. The gas gauge was pointing to "E."

"Stephanie! We're out of gas!"

"You're kidding!" She stared at me, her mascara still smeared from crying.

"I didn't even look at the gas when I got in the car. What should we do?" I racked my brain. We were surrounded by neighborhoods, probably miles from a gas station.

Stephanie started chewing on the ends of her hair. "We are going to get in so much trouble!"

"They don't have to find out!" My Moronic Mood-o-meter was starting to soar. I tried taking deep breaths. "Do you have any money?"

Stephanie checked her wallet. "Six dollars."

I ransacked my purse. "I've got eight. That would buy a few gallons of gas." I threw down my wallet. "How dumb was that, to get in the car and not check the gas!"

I checked my phone. Past midnight. What were we going to do? I could run to a gas station, I guess. Flip flops weren't the greatest running shoes. Leave Stephanie in the car. But I didn't have a gas can. Could I buy one? Was there anyone I could call?

Suddenly it came to me.

"Noah! I'll call Noah!" He was the obvious person.

Stephanie's face brightened. "Great idea, Diana! His mom's house isn't too far away."

"Something happened this afternoon and I was avoiding calling him but ... here goes." My heart started beating more quickly as I tapped in Noah's number.

He picked up. "Hey. I was going to call you." His voice sounded hesitant.

"Yeah, I know. Me too. Right now, listen, it's a really long story but can you bring us some gas?"

He didn't miss a beat. "Where are you?"

Stephanie and I sat in the car, waiting for Noah. A few cars passed, briefly lighting up our faces.

"So ... anyway, what happened to your mom? I thought you were staying with her."

"She left to go to Asheville to meet Barry. She left me at the house with Matt."

"That's crazy. I can't believe she did that."

"Me neither. After coming to get me last night!" Stephanie played with the fringe on her purse. "I was mad at Mama and going behind her back. But, I mean, I didn't know there were no parents at Hunter's party. I didn't know it would be like that."

"Are you okay now?" I searched Stephanie's face as car headlights swept over it.

"When I think about it I want to cry. I feel so stupid. I don't know, I was sitting down there thinking that we might kiss or something."

I couldn't keep it from her any longer. "I kissed Noah today. On the island."

Stephanie's mouth dropped open.

"I know. We both decided it was a mistake. That we're just friends. But I don't know, I'm confused."

"What was it like?"

How to put it into words? When I thought about it a whole vortex of feelings rushed up and whirled around. Made me feel like I was slightly dizzy with a fever. But I probably shouldn't have even brought it up. "I wish I hadn't kissed him," was all I could say.

"What do you mean?"

"Well, it's just so complicated now. I'm nervous about seeing him. Everything was great between us and now there's all this tension."

"Maybe you guys should be more than friends." She smiled for the first time since I'd picked her up.

Noah pulled up behind us in his Jeep. He climbed out lugging a big red gasoline can. He wore a faded Wake Forest T-shirt, and khaki shorts. I jumped out of the car.

"Hey! Oh, thanks for coming!" I glanced at his lips. A wave of nerves hit me. All because of that kiss! I was so mad.

"No problem. Mom's working the night shift tonight and my stepdad was asleep. My stepdad had this can already full for the lawn mower. I'll just have to fill it back up again." Noah shifted the can from one hand to another.

"We can give you money."

"Whatever. I know where you live! Pop your gas tank."

I popped the tank. "I can do it!" I said, reaching for the gas tank.

"No, that's okay." He pulled it away. I watched him unscrew the cap and insert the can's spout into the mouth of the gas tank. He leaned one hand on the trunk as he poured the gas in.

"Hi, Noah!" Stephanie leaned across the driver's seat and waved. "Thanks for coming!" But she didn't get out, and I didn't know whether I was glad or not. I felt so nervous around him now. Did I want to talk to him alone?

"So, what happened?" He fixed his eyes on me and started to laugh.

"Don't laugh at me! It's not funny! I forgot to check how much gas I had."

He laughed again. "Does your grandfather know you have his car?"

"No!"

"So, Diana, you stole your grandfather's car?"

"I didn't steal it! I borrowed it! It was an emergency. I had to get Stephanie."

"So you drove here from the lake house?"

"Yeah." I took a deep breath, thinking about that cop passing me.

"You could've called me to pick her up."

"I was trying to avoid calling you."

He looked at me silently. His face was unreadable in the darkness. The trickle of gas stopped, and he put the gas cap back on. Then, "Why?"

"You know why, Noah!"

He nodded. "Okay. Well, so? What do you want to do?" A car passed, and its headlights shone on his face.

I let my shoulders slump. "I don't know."

"Want to just chill for a while until we figure things out?"

My heart thudded. "Okay."

18

STEPHANIE

Diana and Noah were standing beside the car, having this really intense talk. I tried not to stare at them, but I just couldn't help it. They were facing each other, giving each other the kind of look that you don't usually give somebody unless there's something between you. He was still holding the gas can. I couldn't catch what they were saying. And then they walked away from each other.

Diana came and stood by the driver's side door. "Okay, well. See ya."

"Yeah."

"Thanks again for the gas."

"Yeah."

She got back in the car and Noah's Jeep pulled away, the horn beeping once softly. "Okay," she said, putting on her seatbelt. She started the car. "Back to the lake."

"So what did y'all say?"

"Nothing." She checked for traffic and pulled onto the road.

"Seriously, Diana, what did you say?"

She drove for a minute without answering. "We don't know what we think about ... you know ...

"Kissing?"

"Yeah. We don't know what we think about that. I guess we're going to stop talking for a while."

"Diana! He likes you! You're such a chicken!"

"I don't want to talk about it. I'm driving. I have to concentrate on getting on the highway." We went down the access ramp. There wasn't much traffic.

Diana was afraid to get close to people. She was even afraid of *talking* about being close to people. I hoped Noah wouldn't give up on her.

We drove in silence for a while. I looked out the window at the Charlotte skyline, with the cluster of lit skyscrapers and the stadium. I thought about Diana's kiss with Noah today, which had sounded so romantic.

"Thanks for coming to pick me up."

"No problem." She looked straight ahead, driving.

"We're probably going to get in a lot of trouble."

"Probably."

"I always get in trouble when I hang out with you. And this time it's my own fault." I laughed a little. I let myself relax back against the car seat. I had been so scared sitting there by the mailbox, waiting for Diana. The voices of the kids at the party had floated up from the porch, and I had wanted to put my hands over my ears.

Why had I gone to that party? I felt so bad. I felt like what happened with Hunter was me getting paid back for disobeying Mama.

"I can't wait for you to see Star," Diana was saying. "It was really hard for me to get her to drink from the bottle, but she is crazy for it now. I've given her two bottles, and I'll give her one when we get back. She is so cute! You'll adore her, I promise you."

"Oh, I can't wait to see her. I definitely think I'll like her more than I liked Iggy the iguana."

"I hope Mom and Norm get to see her."

The mention of Daddy and Lynn made us both go silent for a minute. We were driving past Davidson, a small town outside Charlotte. The dark lake glittered on either side of the highway.

What would Daddy and Lynn say about me going to the party? I felt my face get hot just thinking about them knowing.

"Don't tell Daddy and Lynn what happened with Hunter," I said to Diana.

"I won't. I did tell Mom that your mom picked you up, though."

"That's why Daddy tried to call me." My face went hot, and I glanced at my phone. "I didn't answer." Daddy was going to be really mad about what happened.

"Text him when we get to Grandma and Grandpa's," Diana said, glancing away from the road at me. "Just say you're there."

We drove past another town, Mooresville. Neon signs for the movie theatre glowed beside the highway.

"What do you think Daddy and Lynn have talked about with Jon and Olivia?"

"Us. They've probably told them that you're an angel and I'm a devil."

"Oh, come on, Diana!" I started laughing.

"That I'm a big pain in the butt, and they wish they could send me to boarding school or something."

"Maybe they want to send both of us to boarding school!" I laughed again.

We stopped laughing and went silent as the dark highway wound its way north. Soon we'd reached the exit for Grandma and Grandpa's house.

Diana drove down the winding back roads and within minutes we were passing the place she'd hit the deer yesterday. "I swear, when I hit that deer, I never wanted to drive again."

"And you did it for me. I really ... won't forget that."

Diana waved her hand at me. "We don't have to talk about it."

The woods surrounded us on either side, our headlights lighting a path through the darkness. My mind went to a place I didn't want it to go: what if Daddy and Lynn came back and decided to split up.

"Listen, Diana, if Daddy and Lynn decide to split up, we'll still be friends, right?"

Diana didn't answer right away. It was only a few seconds but it seemed longer. "We just have to make sure they don't split up. That's all."

"How can we do that?"

"I don't know."

"I remember being at Grammy's for those weeks when Mama and Daddy were deciding to split up. I thought then that maybe everything had been my fault, and if I had been a more perfect girl that maybe they wouldn't split up."

"But now you know that's not true?"

"In my head I know. Not in my heart."

"So you think that maybe if we're more perfect right now we can keep Mom and Norm from splitting up?"

"Maybe. Except I went to that party and everything. I did just the opposite!"

"It's obvious to me that you're mad at your mom for leaving this weekend."

"But what can we do to keep Daddy and Lynn from splitting up?"

We were both silent, trying to think as we traveled the bends of the winding road. About a block from the cottage, Diana turned off the car lights. "Maybe we can sneak in."

We pulled down the driveway and Diana cut the engine. We sat in the dark driveway for a few seconds, watching the door and listening to the crickets sing. Leaves rustled in a breeze. An owl hooted from a tree nearby.

"Okay, they're still asleep," Diana whispered. "We just have to be really quiet going in." We tried to shut our car doors quietly, and tiptoed across the driveway and up the stairs to the door. Diana slowly turned the knob and pushed the door open an inch at a time. She hung Grandpa's keys on the hook near the refrigerator.

We stood in the dark kitchen. Suddenly, from the sun porch, a sound.

"Maa!"

"Oh, no!"

As Diana raced to the refrigerator and pulled out a bottle, the lamp came on in the family room.

"Diana?" Grandpa's voice, gravelly with sleep.

"Just feeding Star," said Diana, popping the bottle into the microwave.

Grandpa, in his pj's, stepped into the kitchen and blinked at me. "Stephanie? What's going on here?"

Grandma came out into the family room, tying the belt on her bathrobe. "What in the world?"

Diana and I stood together in the kitchen. My arm was barely touching hers. I almost wanted to take her hand, but I didn't. My heart felt like it was going to explode in my throat.

"I went to pick up Stephanie," Diana said boldly.

"I thought she was with her mother!" Grandma exclaimed.

"She met Barry in Asheville," I said in a small voice.

"She left you?" Grandma cried, looking at me.

A wave of shame swept over me, but I also felt justified for being angry with Mama. Grandma thought what she had done was wrong, too.

"You took our car?" Grandpa said. His angry eyes bored into Diana's.

"I had to." There was a tremor in her voice.

The silence in the room was so tense the air seemed to quiver with electricity.

"Without asking permission?" Grandma's voice was high with disbelief.

"I had to!" Diana said. "Stephanie needed me."

"She helped me," I said in a small voice.

"What if something had happened to you, and we didn't even know you were out? What if you had wrecked the car? What if you had both gotten injured, or killed?"

"But nothing happened! We're fine!"

"But if you think about what could have happened, what you did was extremely dangerous," Grandpa said. "We're going to have to tell Lynn and Norm about this, and you're both grounded until they get back tomorrow. I could have gotten up and taken you wherever you needed to go. You deliberately went behind our backs."

There was silence for a few seconds, while that sank in. Then, outside on the sun porch, Star pressed her nose against the glass of the door. "Maa!"

With a sigh, Diana put the bottle in the microwave and turned it on. While the microwave whirred, we all stood in tense silence. It dinged.

"We're sorry," I whispered. "We're really sorry."

Grandpa glanced at me, but then returned his gaze to Diana. His eyes looked wounded. "Why wouldn't you trust us to help you?"

"I don't know," Diana said. "Stephanie was at this party, and she didn't like it there, and she didn't have a ride home. I thought if I asked you I'd get Stephanie in trouble."

"We'll talk about it in the morning," Grandpa said. "For now, get the fawn fed and get to bed." He and Grandma went back to the bedroom and the door shut firmly.

"They're really mad," I whispered to Diana. I was shaking a little.

"Yeah. But I had to do it!"

"I guess you could've asked Grandpa to drive."

"But I didn't." Diana headed for the sun porch. "Come on, Stephanie, meet Star."

Out on the sun porch, I knelt to watch as she held the bottle high and the spotted little fawn turned up her head to drink from it. She was so tiny! I guess I'd always thought fawns were bigger than that. She acted like she was starving, pulling hard on the bottle and making loud smacking noises.

"Wow, look at her drink," I said. Shyly, I held out my hand to pet her neck. "Ooh, her fur feels good. So soft."

"I'm pretty sure I hit her mother," Diana said. "I feel like it's my responsibility to take care of her."

"She seems really attached to you."

Diana seemed pleased. "Yeah, I know."

We played with Star for a few minutes, but she seemed sleepy after eating and soon she had curled up in Diana's lap.

"Are you sleeping down here with her?" I asked her.

"Yeah."

"I will, too. I'll go upstairs and get our pillows and some blankets."

I went up to the room with the white wicker furniture and grabbed a pillow and a blanket for each of us.

I stopped in the bathroom and looked at myself in the mirror. My hair was messed up and mascara streaked my cheeks. I met my own eyes.

A memory flashed, of Hunter heading outside, leaving me alone. I never wanted to talk to Daddy or Mama about what had happened tonight. I was too ashamed.

Then my phone dinged. Who would be texting me this late?

Where are you?

It was from Matt! I'd completely forgotten that he was expecting me to come back to Mama's.

At Diana's grandparents. She picked me up from the party.

You could have texted! I was worried!

Matt was worried about me? I hadn't thought he would. My feelings toward him softened.

Sorry. Thanks for worrying. I'll let you know next time.

Then I turned out the light and tiptoed downstairs.

"Here," I said. Diana and I propped the pillows against the pile of ski vests and spread the blankets over ourselves.

"Maa!" Star snuggled closer to Diana.

I curled under the blanket and fluffed the pillow. Daddy and Lynn would be back for us tomorrow. They'd ask about the party. I would have to tell them why I went. But I didn't really know.

Daddy would find out that Mama had left me with Matt. He'd be mad. He and Mama would have a fight. Everything would be awful.

"I wish tonight had never happened," I said to Diana. I wasn't sure if she was still awake. She lay curled on her side, with Star curled in the space between her knees and chin.

Diana made a "mmmm" sound that she sometimes made when she was falling asleep. Star made a little squeaking sound, breathing in her sleep. I gently stroked her ear with the tips of my fingers. She flicked it.

Outside the sun porch the night creatures buzzed and sang. The dark, mysterious water of the lake was still.

Star sighed and stretched in her sleep. She'd lost her mother, and been lost in the woods with nothing to eat. Now she was in a warm place with bottles to drink, and curled in Diana's arms.

Diana had saved her.

"Good night," I said to Diana.

"Good night," she said.

19

DIANA

I sat in the church pew next to Stephanie. I was wearing one of her stupid sundresses, which was too tight under my arms. Organ music swelled from the front of the church and sunlight poured through the stained glass windows in brilliant reds, greens, and blues.

Grandma and Grandpa sat on the other side of Stephanie.

How had I gotten into this? Even Norm didn't make me go to church. And I hadn't even brought any clothes to wear. But here I was. Because we'd been in so much trouble from last night, when Grandma said we were going, I didn't think I had any way of getting out of it.

This morning, early, I had walked Star around the back yard, while the grass was still wet with dew, with the ski rope around her neck. She had wobbled along on her chopstick legs, staying close. She was incredibly attached to me.

Breakfast had been very quiet. Grandma had made scrambled eggs with cheese in them. Grandpa looked as though he hadn't slept well. Stephanie was like a statue, pale and quiet. I knew I'd betrayed Grandma and Grandpa in going to get Stephanie without telling them.

So, now, here I was in church.

I looked around at all the people. Why were we all here? I wasn't perfect and neither were they, so why were we all here, acting like we were so close to God?

We'd sung some songs whose words had been projected on a large screen in the front of the church. Now the minister, a woman with graying red hair, wearing a dark robe, was getting ready to give her sermon.

My mind floated away to Star. What would the place she was going be like? Would a wild herd of deer accept her into their midst?

"None of us can know the effect or importance of our actions," said the minister. "None of us can know what God wants to use us for. Each of us has to do our best, not knowing what kind of impact we will have."

I stared at Stephanie's leg, next to mine. I glanced over at her face. She believed in all this stuff.

The minister started telling a story, and I found myself listening. "There was a boy who had been in a fire, was in the hospital, and had been out of school for a while. A teacher asked a volunteer if she would go to the hospital and work with the boy on adjectives and adverbs."

That sounded horrible. Being in the hospital would be bad enough, without having to work on adjectives and adverbs on top of it!

The minister went on. "The volunteer went to the hospital and was shocked at how terribly burned the boy was. She didn't think he would survive. What difference do adverbs and adjectives make to this poor boy? she wondered. But she had been asked to work with him, so she did."

Where was the minister going with this story, anyway? It seemed pointless.

"The next day, when the volunteer went back, one of the nurses asked her what she had said the day before. The boy had made a hundred percent improvement. The doctors believed he was going to die, but he had regained his will to live. The volunteer told the nurse she had just worked on adjectives and adverbs.

"Later, after the boy had made more progress, another nurse asked him, 'When did you turn the corner?'

"And he said, 'When that lady came to work with me. I figured they wouldn't send someone to work on adverbs and adjectives with someone who was going to die.' "

The preacher went on with her sermon, but I didn't listen anymore. I was thinking about that volunteer. She'd just done what she'd been asked to do. Nothing special. No big deal. But she'd ended up saving that kid's life. And she didn't even know it.

Huh. Maybe everything we did in our life, every little act, could have a tremendous impact on other living things. In ways that we might not ever know.

I remembered diving into the river while whitewater rafting, and Norm diving after me.

I remembered riding bikes with Cody on the Outer Banks, seeing the foal and her injured mother, and calling the police, and hiding in the dunes while the police came.

I remembered giving Iggy the iguana to the security officer on the cruise ship.

I remembered walking around the hospital floor with Grammy, slowly, talking with her.

I saw Star, coming toward me in the woods. Star, on our sun porch, waiting for her bottle.

I saw Mom, in the car, letting me drive.

I saw Dad, at the Outer Banks, flying with me high over the water.

I saw the disappointed faces of Grandpa and Grandma, this morning, at our quiet breakfast.

And I saw Stephanie, in the passenger seat of the car as I drove last night.

Everything I did mattered. In ways that maybe I would never know.

The minister had finished her sermon. She had her arms high and was blessing the people, saying a prayer.

Stephanie, beside me, wiped her eyes with a tissue.

With that story, something in me had changed.

20

STEPHANIE

Sometimes I cry when I'm in church, when we sing or when the minister tells a story that touches me. I try not to let people see. This week, with everything going on, I was just a mess.

While I was in church, I said a prayer, feeling so thankful that Diana had been able to come and help me out last night. Grandma and Grandpa had been nice to me, and I was thankful for that, but I missed Daddy and Lynn and couldn't wait to get home. I asked God to help me please make things easier for them.

After I said that prayer, I took a deep breath, and felt more peaceful.

As we were getting out of the car after church, suddenly, Diana said, "Grandpa and Grandma, I'm sorry about last night." She closed the car door. "I know how irresponsible it was to take the car like that. I should've asked. It won't happen again."

Grandpa studied her as he put his car keys in his pocket, then put his hand on her shoulder. "I'm glad to hear you say that, young lady. You'll still have to pay the consequences of your actions, but you are forgiven." He smiled, and his eyes seemed full. "We only get angry because we love you so much."

"I know." Diana let him put his arm around her as we went up the wooden porch steps and into the house.

"That's such a relief!" Grandma said, her eyes sparkling. She touched Diana's arm. "Let's have some lunch!"

Diana and I went upstairs to change out of our church clothes. I had worn an old sundress and let Diana borrow the new white sundress Mama had bought me yesterday, because it was the only one that fit her. Though it was just a little short.

"Thanks for the dress," she said, handing it to me.

"Do you want it? It fits you."

She considered. "No. If I go back to church, they'll just have to put up with me in my blue jeans. But what did you think of that story the minister told, about the boy who was burned?"

"It made me cry. Why?"

She shrugged. Had it touched her too?

After we set the table for Grandma, Diana warmed the goat's milk, and I went out to the sun porch with her. Star struggled to her feet and tottered over to us.

"Maa!"

And then she licked my arm! Her little tongue was warm and smooth. "Hey, can I try giving the bottle to her?"

"Sure." Diana handed me the bottle. "Just hold it up and kind of move it back and forth."

I found I had to hold tight to the bottle. Star was so eager she almost pulled the bottle out of my hand. I pulled back on it, then gave it to her a little, then pulled back again.

"That's good," Diana said.

"Aww. Look," I said. I watched the way her beautiful almond-shaped eyes closed as she drank. I stroked the edge of her pear-shaped ear, feeling the softness of her fur.

"Look at her face. Isn't it beautiful?" Diana said.

"Yeah. Don't you wish we could keep her?"

"Yeah."

As Star finished the bottle, we laughed at the smeary places she had left on the windows by pressing her round nose to the glass.

"Come on, girls, time for lunch!" Grandma called.

We washed our hands and sat down with Grandma and Grandpa to a huge meal of salad, watermelon, and fried chicken that we'd picked up on the way home from church. When Grandpa suggested that we have a blessing, Diana joined hands without rolling her eyes the way she usually did. We bowed our heads. I was holding hands with Grandma on one side and Grandpa on the other.

"Dear Lord," he said. "Thank you for the chance to spend time with our granddaughters and to share their lives."

Warmth washed through me. He was calling me his granddaughter!

"Thank you for bringing Diana and Stephanie back safe to us last night. Help us to find a home for that little fawn. Thank you for this wonderful meal before us. For these and all our many blessings, amen."

"Amen," Grandma and I repeated. Grandma squeezed my hand.

And then, a second later, Diana said, "Amen."

If Grandma and Grandpa noticed, they didn't say anything.

"Well, we'll address the consequences for last night

when your parents get here," Grandpa said as he passed the watermelon. "Meanwhile, it's a beautiful day for kneeboarding. Stephanie, want to give it another try?"

Diana grinned at me. "Sure she does, Grandpa! You were so close, Steph, you can't give up!"

My heart beat hard a few times. No, I didn't want to give up. Besides, Daddy would be proud of me if I told him I could kneeboard. "Okay!" I said. "I'll try again."

"That's what I like to hear!" Grandpa said, clapping his hands together. "I'll go down and get the boat ready after lunch."

"Diana, do you want to invite your friend Noah over to ski this afternoon since he rushed off without getting a chance to yesterday?" Grandma asked.

"Oh, no, that's okay," Diana said quickly, with a quick glance at me.

After lunch, while we were helping Grandma clean up, Grandpa went down to the dock to get the boat ready, but was back within a few minutes.

"Come down and look!" he said, cracking the screen door and popping his head in.

"What? What?" said Grandma.

"I'm not going to tell you, you have to come see for yourself," Grandpa said. "Hurry up!"

"Oh, I know, I know what it is! Oh, my, come on girls, let's go!" Grandma's voice got high and excited as she untied her apron and tossed it on the counter.

"Hurry up!" said Grandpa.

We dropped our dish towels and all followed Grandpa down through the back yard to the dock. And there, on the pontoon boat cover, sat the mother goose, and peeking from underneath her breast was one puffy little yellowish gray gosling, cheeping with all its might. The mother gazed at us with beady black eyes, a broad chest and obvious pride.

"Shhh! Don't scare her!" Grandpa said. "Stay back."

Small pieces of the broken eggs surrounded the mother. Just behind the mother, two more goslings struggled to get themselves hatched. The tops of the eggs were gone and they strained with their necks and wings to wiggle free. Their feathers were wet and slick against their tiny heads and stumpy wings. Their cheeping was constant, like a soft whistling.

"Will you look at that?" Grandma said. "Look what hard work it is to get hatched!" She and Grandpa stood and watched, holding hands. Not far away, the father goose swam around, peering at his newborn family and calling to them.

We were transfixed while the fluffy one cheeped at its mother and the other two gradually wiggled out of their eggs. The mother stood up, flapping her wings, and we saw four more broken eggs underneath her, all with little wet heads making their way out.

"Seven little goslings!" Grandpa said.

The mother nosed the babies with her beak, as if checking on them and counting.

"Like a miracle!" said Grandma.

We decided to give the geese some privacy, so, not long afterward, we took the boat out on the choppy water. Diana helped me with the clasps on the ski vest. Grandpa, at the wheel of the boat, turned toward us.

"Okay, Miss Stephanie, you're going to get up this time," he said. "Everything's going to come together."

"Yeah, it's going to be great!" Diana said.

"I hope so!" Taking a deep breath, I dove in, the cool water soothing on my hot skin. The sun reflected in bright prisms from the surface of the water, making the water look as though it was sprinkled with glitter.

I treaded water while Diana tossed the kneeboard to me, letting it skim across the surface, and then threw me the ski rope.

"Remember what to do?" Diana yelled.

"I think so!" I placed my fingers carefully on the handle.

Grandpa gave the boat a little gas to put tension in the ski rope. "Ready?"

"Ready!"

He hit the throttle and the boat took off. I centered my body on the board, then got one knee, then the other, in place. The board felt slippery underneath me, but I managed not to fall. Slowly, I let myself straighten up.

"Lean back!" Diana shouted.

I did, carefully, without disturbing my balance. And all of a sudden, I was kneeboarding! The water flew by at breakneck speed. The air blew into me and rushed past. I held onto the rope, my hair flying out behind me, feeling the pull in my arms.

"Ya-hoo! " Diana yelled, holding both thumbs way up.

"Way to go!" yelled Grandpa.

"Whoo-hoo!" I was flying along with this gigantic grin on my face!

I held on for dear life, keeping my eye on the boat ahead of me. Gradually I relaxed a little bit, and started looking around, at the wake unfurling beside me, at the glittering water, at the blue sky, and the houses and docks flashing by.

I was really kneeboarding! I drew a deep breath of satisfaction.

Should I try to cross the wake? The water behind the boat was churned up but the water on the other side of the wake was smooth.

I decided to try.

I pulled the ski rope to the right and leaned slightly right. I inched closer to the wake. I leaned a little more, and soon was next to it. It churned along, a roiling hump or wave, on both sides behind the boat, like a "v."

I leaned to the right just a little more, to see if I could slide over it and bam! The board slid out from under me and I wiped out, face-first in the water.

I came up, my face stinging, as the rope went skittering away.

The boat immediately began to circle back for me. I treaded water, realizing just how tired and shaky my arms were.

"Want to go again?" Grandpa asked as he drove up.

I shook my head. "I'll come in."

"Good try." Diana helped me climb up the ladder into the back of the boat.

"I was trying to cross the wake." I collapsed, water streaming everywhere, into one of the back seats, taking off the ski vest.

"Yeah, we could tell. You'll get the hang of that next time."

"The important thing is you were up!" Grandpa held his hand out to give me a high five. "Way to go!"

"I know!" I grinned at him, feeling dizzy with success.

After that, I wrapped myself in a big towel and let the sun warm my hair and face while I watched Diana kneeboard and then slalom ski. She zipped across the wake, out beside the boat, and then boomeranged back around to the other side of the boat. She even did a three-sixty, showing off for me and Grandpa.

Finally, she clambered back into the boat, dripping and out of breath, and she dropped into the other back seat. "Whoo! That was awesome!"

"Good job, Diana," Grandpa said, as he turned the wheel, heading back for home. "Hey, looks like somebody is standing out on our dock. And it's not Grandma."

Diana and I looked over and sure enough, someone was standing there. He wore blue striped board shorts and held a black wakeboard.

Diana's mouth dropped open.

21

DIANA

Oh man, what was Noah doing here? I thought about yesterday and felt my cheeks go hot.

Grandpa cut the motor so we wouldn't disturb the mother goose and her goslings, and we glided up next to the dock.

"Caramba!" Noah said.

I started laughing.

"You invited me to come back and wakeboard, so I thought I'd take you up on it." Noah held up his wakeboard.

"Come aboard!" Grandpa said.

Noah handed Stephanie his wakeboard and I grabbed his hand as he climbed on board. It felt electric when our hands touched. I tried to read his eyes, feeling a little breathless.

"It looks like you have some baby geese there on top of your pontoon boat!" Noah said.

"How about that, isn't that great?" Grandpa said. "Wow, that's a serious wakeboard, young man."

"Yessir, I plan on doing some serious wakeboarding."

"All right, then."

Grandpa drove up to the larger section of the cove to give Noah plenty of room. "How fast do you like to go, Noah?" Grandpa asked.

"About twenty?"

"All right. Let's see what you can do!"

"Yessir!" Noah put on a vest, tossed his wakeboard onto the water, and dove after it.

Stephanie touched my arm and whispered in my ear. "Don't be nervous. He likes you!"

"Ready?" Grandpa called to Noah.

"Hit it!" Noah yelled.

And Grandpa took off, and Noah put on a show. He popped out of the water, jumped high over the wake, and then started carving the choppy water adjacent to the boat. He then did a three-sixty while skiing back over the wake in the other direction. Then he jumped over the wake, high in the air, landed with a splash and kept on going. Wow, he was amazing!

He landed jump after jump, with Stephanie and me sitting in the back of the boat cheering for him. On one jump, he tried to turn a complete flip, and wiped out. But he came up laughing. After that, I skied again, and then Stephanie tried kneeboarding again, and she even managed to cross the wake before she wiped out.

When we were all completely worn out, wrapped in towels and lying across the boat seats, Grandpa brought us in, and we tied up the boat. Grandma met us on the dock, and we sat out there soaking in the sun, taking breaks to jump in the water and cool off every now and then. The floating dock creaked and rocked under us, making us so relaxed it was hard to stay awake. Noah was lying beside me on a towel on the dock, and when I closed my eyes I got goosebumps thinking about how close he was.

Stephanie was watching us, meeting my eyes and raising her eyebrows and giving me meaningful smiles. I was trying to ignore her.

Part of me wished I could just get a few minutes alone with Noah, and part of me was avoiding it.

The goslings, only a few hours old, were all fluffy now, with grayish-yellow down and little beige beaks.

They cheeped constantly, scooting around their mom, who remained sitting stoically on the nest and nuzzling them.

I was dying to pick one up, but thought I better not try with the mother and father goose so watchful.

"Let's leave them alone for now, though I don't know how they're going to get down from that boat cover," Grandpa said. "We may need to give them a little help once they're ready to leave the nest."

"When will that be?" Stephanie asked.

"I have no idea!" Grandpa said.

Noah was extremely polite to Grandma and Grandpa, saying, "sir," and "ma'am." Then Grandma gave him one of her famous interviews.

"Where do you think you want to go to college, Noah?"

"Well, my older brother goes to Wake Forest, so ... " Noah kind of trailed off. "I'm not sure. I guess I'll just have to see where I get in."

"Grandpa taught at Wake Forest," I said.

"Oh, really?"

"For thirty years," Grandpa said proudly.

"What did you teach?" Noah asked.

"Physics."

"Whoa. I'm supposed to take Physics next year. My brother said it was a bear."

"What's your brother majoring in, Noah?" Grandma asked.

"I don't think he's decided."

I could tell Noah was starting to squirm. "Hey, come see the fawn," I said.

"Sure!"

As we headed up through the back yard, I sneaked glances at Noah. His wet hair was starting to wave as it dried, and his silver earring glinted in the afternoon sun. In the kitchen, as I grabbed a bottle and heated it up, I felt hyperaware of him standing next to me, watching.

"Wow," he said as he followed me out onto the sun porch. "You all sure have a lot of wildlife around here."

"Maa!" Star tottered toward me the minute I came in with the bottle.

Stephanie joined us, and then we all sat on the floor, watching while Star drank her bottle, pulling hard.

"She's so enthusiastic!" Noah said, laughing.

"I know! Isn't she cute?" Stephanie said.

She drained the bottle in no time, and then we walked Star around the yard.

"So," Noah asked, as we strolled through the grass, glancing at Grandma in the kitchen window. "You guys in trouble for taking the car?"

"Yeah, we're grounded," Stephanie said.

"Nice to go kneeboarding and have a friend over while you're grounded!"

"Yeah!" I said. "You didn't give them much of a choice since you just showed up."

"Hey, they invited me yesterday!" Noah said.

As we came around from the back to the side yard, gravel crunched as a dark blue pickup truck pulled into our driveway. A pretty lady with blonde hair wearing overalls climbed out of the driver's seat. "Hi, I'm Kirsten, the wildlife rehabilitator."

My heart pounded once, hard. I had known this was coming, but I was filled with dread. She seemed really nice. I realized I had been hoping I could come up with reasons not to let her see Star. "Hi, I'm Diana, the one who called you."

"So this is your orphaned fawn! What a sweetie!" She immediately came over and knelt next to Star, rubbing her hands over Star's ears and face. Star licked her cheek. "They like the taste of salt on our skin," Kirsten said. She ran her hands over Star, expertly checking for injuries.

"Oh!" I knelt, too. "I thought she was being affectionate toward me."

"No, sorry, it's just the salt," Kirsten said, with a laugh. "This fawn looks to be about a week old. Really young. And you waited for the mother to come back?"

"Yeah, I found her in the woods and brought her

home, but then took her back and waited almost a whole day."

Kirsten nodded, looking at me with kind brown eyes. "See, usually the mothers will have two babies. And they will stash them, a little distance apart, at dawn. They put them in a different place every day. And the does will be gone for most of the day, and then come back at dusk."

"Her mother didn't come back. I waited."

"Maybe something happened to the mother."

"I hit a deer when I was driving the day before I found her. It was near where she was. I thought it might have been her mother. It didn't fall down when I hit it. It kept running."

Kirsten's eyes widened. "That could be. It might have had a lot of adrenalin in its system and been able to run a long distance with injuries." Kirsten smiled and ran her palm over Star's head. "But she didn't make it back. You probably saved this fawn's life."

A warm feeling coursed through me.

Just then Grandpa and Grandma came out onto the porch, and I introduced them to Kirsten.

"She's been giving the fawn a bottle of goat's milk every three hours or so, just like we read online," Grandpa said.

"Great. She looks good. You've done a good job,"

Kirsten said, with a smile that crinkled the skin beside her eyes.

I wanted to stall for time. "So, how many fawns have you taken care of?"

"Oh, dozens and dozens." Kirsten went to the back of the truck and pulled out a large dog carrier and set it on the ground. "Sometimes I'm taking care of as many as eight or nine fawns at once."

"How long do you keep them?"

"I keep them about a week. Then I pass them on to another rehabilitator who keeps them a little longer, and gets them on goat chow and sweet feed, and then releases them into the wild. They join existing herds."

"Do the other herd members attack the new ones? I learned that horses sometimes do that."

"No, deer aren't like that. They don't pick on a new member. They welcome them."

"Oh, that's good." I racked my brain for more questions. She was going to put Star in that carrier and take her. I swallowed. "I can come to visit her, right?"

Kirsten's eyes softened, and she looked down quickly. "No, Diana, I'm sorry, you can't. Fawns imprint really easily on humans. She is following you like a dog, so it looks like she might have already imprinted on you. We need for her to have only one caretaker, and that has to be me. So, you'll have to say your good-byes now, I'm afraid."

Tears sprang to my eyes.

"You mean I'll never see her again?"

Kirsten's eyes teared a little now, too. "No, you won't."

I felt like sobbing. It wasn't just saying good-bye to Star. It was everything.

"Listen, you're doing the right thing, Diana." Kirsten put her hand gently on my arm. "It's illegal to keep a deer as a pet. This way she'll be in good hands and she'll find a herd to belong to."

I knelt and took Star's little body in my arms, feeling the beat of her heart in her chest. I touched some of the delicate, star-like white spots that lined her backbone and spread over her flanks. She stared at me with those almond eyes framed with the long lashes. Now I couldn't stop the crying. "Bye, Star." She nuzzled and licked the side of my face. Just for the salt, according to Kirsten. "You be good, now."

I glanced up at Stephanie and saw that she was crying, too. So were Grandma and Grandpa. I couldn't even look at Noah.

My vision was blurred as Kirsten put Star in the carrier and shut the door. "All set, then." Kirsten put the carrier in the truck's passenger seat.

"Maa!" said Star.

My heart jumped. I balled my hands into fists.

"Thanks for calling me. She's in good hands,"

Kirsten said as she began to back out of the driveway. I followed her to the end of the driveway and watched as the blue truck wound around the corner and out of sight.

I wiped my nose on the end of my t-shirt as I headed back down the driveway. Grandma took my face in her hands and kissed me on the forehead.

"You did a good thing, Diana."

"I better get going," Noah said. He picked up his wake board from the porch where he'd left it.

Grandma and Grandpa and Stephanie told Noah good-bye and left the two of us out by the driveway alone. Noah leaned against the porch stairs. "I'm sorry you're so sad about the fawn."

"I know it was the right thing. I'll get over it. I just . . . I don't know." I wiped my nose with the back of my hand. "I'm sorry to be so upset."

"Don't be. I like that about you. You get so into stuff."

"Oh. Thanks." I felt my cheeks flush with pleasure.

"Okay, well, I guess I'll see you?"

I looked into his face, feeling a little out of breath. "I thought we weren't going to talk. And now here you showed up today. What's that about?"

He shrugged. "Maybe yesterday wasn't a mistake. Maybe we can hang out over the summer and see how it goes." He bumped the wake board against his leg nervously a couple of times. "No pressure. What do you think?"

"No pressure?" That sounded pretty good.

Then he touched his index finger to the end of my nose. "No pressure."

After he left, Stephanie and I went inside and cleaned up the sun porch. Moronic Mood-o-Meter zooming around at about a nine. "You were right. He likes me. But he says no pressure." I dipped the mop in the bucket of vinegar and water to swab the floor.

"Awesome, Diana!" Stephanie was collecting the towels to put in the laundry. "That is so great!"

I wrung out the mop, and swabbed one section. "I thought he liked you at first."

"No, look at the way he came out last night to bring you gas." Stephanie went behind me, drying the floor with one of the towels. "Noah really cares about you."

As I mopped another section of the floor, I said, "In the past, with guys, I've kind of messed things up. I don't want that to happen this time."

"It won't," Stephanie said. "You've changed. You're more caring. You risked getting in trouble last night to come and help me out. Honestly, I'll never forget that."

I leaned on the mop, letting her words sink it. It felt like the sun was warming my face.

"I feel like, no matter what happens with Daddy and

Lynn, you and I will always be close. We'll always be sisters."

I felt tears pricking at the corners of my eyes. Would I ever have believed that this could happen, back when we were first together at the ranch?

I closed my eyes, letting a few moments spin by in silence.

"But there's something else I've been wondering about," Stephanie was saying. I opened my eyes.

"What?"

"Do you remember when Kirsten picked up Star, she said that usually the mother deer has two fawns?" Stephanie looked at me with fearful eyes. "Do you think there might be another fawn out there in the woods? Waiting for the mother to come back?"

I stared at Stephanie and caught my breath. Why hadn't I thought of that? "There might! We have to go check!"

22

STEPHANIE

The late afternoon sun was skimming the tops of the trees, low in the sky, as Diana and I raced down the road to the place she had first found Star. Our flip flops made loud smacks on the asphalt as we ran.

"It was near a pine tree missing some bark on the trunk, right by the edge of the woods," Diana said, out of breath. "Right around here." She angled into the woods, ducking under some branches and knocking others aside. I followed her, the sharp pine smell enveloping me. "She was kind of underneath a bush, where you couldn't see her."

We crashed through the underbrush, bending down and searching low under every bush we saw. I was peeking under some low-hanging branches when Mama's ring tone sounded on my phone. My heart started pounding, but I didn't pick up. She had left me and gone to Asheville. She could just worry.

The ringtone stopped.

"Wasn't that your phone?" Diana said from a few yards away. "Why didn't you answer it?"

"It's Mama. I don't feel like talking to her right now."

Diana wound around a few pine trees, searching. "Seems like you're pretty mad at her."

I didn't answer. I just wandered a bit deeper into the woods. "Do you think we're getting too far away from where you found Star?"

Diana stopped and looked back out at the road. "Maybe. Let's head that way."

We headed back toward the tree missing the bark, slowly, and began to make concentric circles to try to make sure we'd covered all the ground.

"Your mom isn't going to change," Diana said. Our feet made silky hushing sounds as we rambled through the pine needles. "You're always giving me such a hard time about not forgiving people. But it seems like you can't forgive your mom."

Diana's words echoed in my head as I continued on the search. Thinking about what had happened with Mama, my blood pounded in my temples. I realized how mad I still was. But when would I learn? That was just the way Mama was.

Maybe Diana was right. Maybe she wasn't going to change. Maybe I needed to follow the advice I was always giving Diana about forgiving people. Maybe I needed to forgive Mama. I drew a deep breath. I'd call her back tonight.

Finally, after twenty minutes of searching, Diana threw up her hands. "Well, I give up. It was a good idea, anyway, Steph."

"Okay." I followed her winding route toward the edge of the woods, scanning the ground. Diana was already standing in the open when I decided to look under one last small bush beside a rotting tree trunk.

And there, rising to its feet, was a tiny fawn even smaller than Star. With a gasp, I knelt, pulling back stray branches.

Its deep brown eyes looked at me searchingly. Its pear-shaped ears pricked anxiously in my direction.

I jumped to my feet. "Diana! Come here!"

I knelt again, examining the fawn. It held one of its hind legs off the ground, not putting weight on it.

Diana was beside me, staring. "Stephanie, you were right! Oh, my gosh, she's probably starving."

"And there's something wrong with her leg."

"Maybe." Without hesitating, Diana reached under the branches and gently pulled the fawn out. It struggled, crying weakly. Diana clasped the little body to her chest, with the legs hanging down. "Come on!" She ran toward the house.

I followed. I couldn't believe we had found another fawn!

We pounded through the yard and up onto the porch.

"Grandma! Grandpa!" Diana yelled. I opened the door and we burst into the kitchen.

Grandma came into the kitchen. "Oh, goodness! Not another one!"

Grandpa came from the back bedroom. "What's going on?"

"Get a bottle ready, Stephanie!" Diana said. "Hurry!"

My hands shook as I poured the goat's milk into one of the bottles that Grandma had just rinsed, put it into the microwave, and turned it on.

Grandma grabbed blankets and towels from the laundry room, lay them on the floor of the sun porch, and Diana gently laid the fawn on them. The fawn scrambled to its feet, bleating softly, standing unevenly on three legs.

"She's starving!" Diana said.

"Well, we know what to do this time around," Grandpa said.

I brought the bottle out on the sun porch, shaking it to mix it.

"Can I try?" I said. "Since I found her?"

Diana nodded. "Okay." And then she started giving me all kinds of instructions.

"Okay, okay!" I tried letting the milk drip on her nose, and pushing the nipple between the fawn's lips. Her little round black nose sniffed at me and at the goat's milk.

"We need to call Kirsten again before she gets too far down the road," Grandpa said. "She'll need to come back."

"Okay," Diana said.

I kept trying to feed her while Diana tapped in the number she'd left on the pad on the counter. She got Kirsten right away.

"We found another one! We have her here on the sun porch. But she's only putting weight on three legs. There's definitely something wrong." Diana listened, then scribbled something down. She hung up. "Kirsten says the leg might be broken. She says she'll meet us at the vet's office. She gave me the address."

Suddenly, the fawn started to suck on the nipple voraciously.

"She's got it! She's got it!" She suckled eagerly and loudly, making loud gasping sounds.

"Look at that poor little thing," said Grandma.

"She's so beautiful. What should we name her?" Diana asked.

"What about Clover?" I said.

"I like that," said Grandma.

"Well, we better get her over to the vet's office," Grandpa said. "Somebody will need to hold her in their lap."

Grandpa drove with Grandma in the front seat, Diana and me in the back, and Clover on Diana's lap on a towel. Diana kept her arms wrapped around her. Clover struggled occasionally, but her injured leg prevented her from moving too much.

Twenty minutes later we pulled into the gravel parking lot of the emergency veterinary clinic, which was a double-wide trailer. Kirsten was already there, with Star still in the dog carrier in her truck. She came up to our car window, and leaned in.

"There's a new vet here today that I've never worked with before, but he seems very good. He said to bring the fawn right in. Want me to carry her?"

"Since I found her, can I?" I asked.

"Sure."

I ran around the side of the car and wrapped my arms around Clover's little body, hugging her close the way I'd seen Kirsten do with Star.

"Maa!" As I held her in the waiting room, I could feel her heart beating next to mine. She struggled a little. Her ears, twitching back and forth, tickled my chin.

The vet, with graying dark hair and kind eyes behind glasses, hurried out, wearing blue scrubs. "Hey, I'm Dr. Miller. Come on back and let's take a look."

We all went into the exam room, and Dr. Miller directed me to place Clover on the metal exam table. I put her down, and her little hooves slid on the slippery metal. With gentle hands, Dr. Miller examined Clover, who winced and kicked when he touched the swollen area on her leg. "It feels like it might be a break. We'll need to get some x-rays to find out for sure." He suggested we take a seat out in the waiting room for a few minutes.

When he called us back into the exam room a few minutes later, Dr. Miller pointed to the x-rays hanging up on a light screen. "It's definitely broken." Dr. Miller traced the ghostly image of Clover's bone with his pen. "Can you see the fracture there? It'll have to be set. What I'd like to do is start an IV and get the fawn stabilized, and then I'll do surgery later today or tomorrow." He adjusted his glasses, looking at Kirsten.

"That would be great," Kirsten said, with a shy smile. "Thank you so much. Not many vets would be willing to work on a fawn."

"Well, a broken bone is a broken bone, and I enjoy

orthopedic surgery," said Dr. Miller. "And then you can come pick her up in a couple of days, if she's doing well."

"Perfect," Kirsten said, her smile broadening.

"Our staff will love having a fawn here," Dr. Miller said. "That doesn't happen too often. This little girl is lucky you kids found her. Good work!"

Diana poked me in the arm, and I felt myself blush.

The technician came to take Clover.

"Wait. Will we see her again?" I asked. We had only had her for a little while. How could I have developed such affection in such a short time?

Kirsten shook her head. "No, so sorry. I'll pick her up once the surgery is done and take her to rehabilitate her at my place. Remember, you're not allowed to visit. I can call you with updates."

So, once again, Diana and I said our good-byes.

"Bye, little girl," Diana said, stroking her head. "They're going to make you all well." We each gave Clover a kiss on the top of the head. Then the technician took Clover from us.

"Maa!" she bleated, as she was carried out of the room.

The four of us were quiet part of the way home.

"Star and Clover will be taken care of and eventually be reintroduced to the wild," Grandma said.

"When can we call to check on them?" Diana asked.

"Maybe tomorrow afternoon?" Grandpa said.

Once we arrived back at Grandma and Grandpa's cottage, Mama's ring tone started up on my phone again. Diana gave me a pointed look.

"You should answer it."

I tightened my lips and nodded. A prickly feeling ran up my spine. I walked through the grassy back yard and down to the dock so I could have privacy.

"Hi, Mama."

Shadows stretched over the graying planks and the dock rocked up and down. While the father goose swam in alert semi-circles around the dock, the mother goose rearranged herself in the nest, touching her bill to each of the fluffy goslings as they quietly cheeped around her.

"Hi, sugar. How are you doing? I've been thinking about you all day."

"Really?" I caught my breath, then closed my eyes and shook my head. I wasn't going to let myself be taken in.

"Did everything go all right with you and Matt last night?"

I considered what to tell her. I started to say everything had been fine, but then I changed my mind. "I need to talk to you about that."

"Oh, well, okay, we can talk when I get home, sugar.

Barry and I had such a lovely time. I got here in time to go to a place where we did some dancing. It meant a lot to him for me to come, I think."

My heart beat hard a few times. I remembered Diana telling me to forgive Mama. "Well, that's good. I'm glad."

"Thanks for understanding, sugar."

"Sure. No problem." I looked out over the surface of the water, where the sunlight seemed to glitter. The baby geese cheeped.

"So, I'll be home later tonight. Will you still be at the house when I get back?"

"No, Daddy and Lynn are going to pick me up this afternoon."

Mama hesitated. "Well, all right. I understand. I'll miss seeing you tonight!"

"Me, too. And we have to talk ... next week when I see you."

I hung up. I watched the baby geese, thinking about how hard they'd had to work to crack out of those shells.

23

DIANA

Stephanie and I were packed and ready to go, hanging out on the dock with Grandma and Grandpa, waiting for Mom and Norm. Stephanie had been quiet since she talked to her mom, but I hadn't had a chance to talk to her about it.

Grandpa's arm was around Grandma, and we were watching the baby geese.

"Look at them jockeying for position," Grandma said.

The goslings jostled the mother and each other as

they tumbled around the nest. The warmth of the after-noon sun made me feel so lazy that when one of the goslings climbed over the feathery curve of the nest and waddled around on the boat cover, I didn't move from where I was stretched out on the dock. I watched sleepily as the gosling toddled over to the edge of the cover, took one more step, and blip! It fell over the side, landing in the water between the boat and the slip.

"Oh, no!" I yelled, jumping to my feet.

The father goose immediately swam over and began to honk. The mother waddled to the edge of the boat cover and peered down, calling out.

"Good night, Miss Agnes!" said Grandpa, getting up.

I raced over and lay down on the warm boards, peering at the shifting water next to the boat. Wavelets lapped at the boat's sides, and at first I couldn't even see the gosling, but when I leaned over farther I saw it flailing. Starting to float to the shadowed water under the dock.

Everyone had crowded beside the boat next to me, trying to see.

"Can you see it? Can you reach it?" Grandma called.

I stretched my fingertips as far as I could, but the baby had floated too far for me to reach. I scrambled over the edge, feet-first, chest-deep in the water, and swam one stroke over to the struggling gosling. Water streamed off its fluffy little head as I scooped my hands underneath it and swept it onto the dock. It immediately shook itself off, frantically cheeping.

"You got it, you got it!" Grandma's voice was filled with relief.

Grandpa leaned down and picked it up. "Okay, little guy, we gotcha. Good save there, Diana!"

I waded over to the steps and Grandma handed me a towel, which I wrapped around me, wet clothes and all.

"I think we better move these goslings so more don't fall off." Grandpa carried the gosling down the length of the dock and set it gently in the grass, where it waddled in a circle, cheeping. "Who wants to help me move these little guys?"

"Oh, I want to!" I said, dropping my towel.

"Okay, let's get to work. Watch out for Mama and Papa."

But, for whatever reason, the mother and father did not protest us picking up the babies. When we approached the boat cover, the mother cocked her head at us but wasn't aggressive. The father flapped his wings, but did not come any closer. Grandpa talked to them in a soothing way, then carefully picked up two more babies that had wandered near the edge of the boat cover, and strode with them to the end of the dock and placed them in the grass.

Being careful not to get close to the mother, I picked up two more babies.

"Oh, they're so soft!" I followed Grandpa as they squirmed and cheeped in my hands. Kneeling in the grass, I gently put them down. Grandma came right behind me, with two more, and set them down carefully.

Stephanie ventured near the nest, but when the mother cocked her head and fixed her beady eyes on her, she hesitated. I went back and, over the mother's protestations, cradled that last one as I walked down the dock, and placed it in the grass next to its brothers and sisters.

"Now," said Grandpa, crossing his arms over his chest. "We've got to hope the mother comes to join them."

The goslings toddled around in the grass in aimless circles, and their cheeping grew louder.

"Go on over there now, Mama," Grandma said. "Maybe we shouldn't stand so close."

We walked a short distance away from the babies and stood in the yard, watching and waiting. She stood anxiously on the nest, stretching her neck in the direction of her babies, and calling to them. We thought she would never go to them.

"Come on, Mama. Come get your babies," I said.

"Soon as she moves, maybe I'll move the nest to a safer spot," Grandpa said.

We stood and waited, holding our breath.

A car's engine sounded from the driveway.

"Mom and Norm are here," I said. I met Stephanie's eyes, and we didn't have to say a thing, because I knew what she was thinking. Leaving the babies, we headed up to the house.

"We're back!" Mom called, as she climbed, stretching, from the driver's seat. I quickly searched her face.

Norm got out of the passenger seat and shut the door.

"Hello, hello!" Grandpa said, raising both arms in greeting. "How was it?"

"Fine," Norm said noncommittally. Stephanie stood by the porch, watching him.

I knew just how she felt. Could I figure out by the way Mom's face looked, by the way she moved, by the way she looked at us, and at Norm, how things had gone? I watched them both.

"Stephanie?" Norm said. "Lynn told me last night you were with your mother. But now you're back here?"

"Yeah."

"Come on in," Grandma said quickly. "Are you hungry? I can fix you some soup."

"No, no, we'll eat at home," Mom said. She looked at me. "Diana, why are your clothes all wet?"

"I had to save a gosling."

Everything was suddenly quiet as we trooped into the kitchen. I didn't know what Grandpa and Grandma would say. Our stuff was on the couch, packed and ready. Would Norm put his arm around Mom? Sometimes he did that, when things were good. Put his arm around her and played with her hair. But they didn't touch each other.

Mom looked expectantly at Grandma and Grandpa. "So?"

I held my breath. Then, I decided not to be a coward. I stood up straight and looked Norm right in the eye. "I took the car last night. Without asking."

Norm knitted his brows and Mom's mouth dropped open. "You what?"

"Go ahead and ground me." I crossed my arms over my chest, then glanced at Grandpa, expecting to see a stern expression.

Mom crossed her arms too. "Whoa, hold on, here!"

"She was trying to help me," Stephanie said quickly. "She came to pick me up because I was stuck at a party."

"How did that happen?" Norm fixed Stephanie with a stare.

"I thought I had a ride but ... I didn't."

"Where was your mother?"

"She ... met Barry in Asheville."

Norm's mouth dropped open. "No wonder you didn't pick up your phone when I called," Norm said.

"Maybe we should sit down for this," Grandma said.

Grandpa put one arm around me and the other around Stephanie. "We've had quite a weekend. I think you should discuss this as a family. I trust the girls to tell the truth about what happened, and you two to decide what you'll do."

"Let me get this straight, Stephanie," Norm said, his voice rising. "Your mother came and picked you up . . . and then left you to go to Asheville to meet Barry?"

Stephanie nodded, looking at the floor.

Norm looked like he was ready to explode.

Mom put her hand on Norm's arm. "Honey, let's talk about that later."

I decided it was a good time to go upstairs and change into dry clothes.

When I got back downstairs, Norm's face had gone back to its regular color and everyone was talking in normal voices. Stephanie and I headed out to the car with our stuff.

"Can we check on the goslings before we go?" I said. We headed down through the yard, and there we saw the mother leading the babies through the grass, single file, cheeping and waddling, with the father at the end, making sure no one was left behind.

"They came for them!" I said.

"Aren't they darling?" Grandma said.

Minutes later Stephanie and I sat in the back seat of Norm's car and we were backing out the driveway.

Norm drove and Mom held a big bag of Grandpa's tomatoes. Grandma and Grandpa stood on the porch, waving. I had given them both an extra long hug good-bye. Grandpa had his arm around Grandma. Their white hair shone in the late afternoon sun.

"I'll grate the cheese," I said to Stephanie. "You cut up the tomatoes."

Stephanie stood next to me at the counter with the cutting board. We'd set the table, and lined up bowls for the ingredients for fajitas. Sour cream, lettuce, taco sauce, black beans, chicken strips, and shells stood on the counter.

"Need any help?" Mom poked her head around the corner.

"No, no! We're doing it, Mom. You and Norm relax!"

Mom looked skeptical, but nodded. "Okay, then. Let me know if you change your mind!" Mom's head disappeared as she headed back to the family room. I heard the murmur of her voice as she told Norm that we didn't want any help.

"The directions for cooking the chicken are on the back of the fajitas packet," Stephanie said.

"You read and I'll follow them."

This was Stephanie's and my plan to keep Mom and Norm together. We'd make them a nice dinner, and then we'd each make a speech telling them how much it meant to us to be a family. Our cooking abilities were pretty much limited to spaghetti and fajitas, and we'd decided on fajitas.

Stephanie and I were both grounded for two weeks, and I lost driving privileges. Noah understood and said he'd see me when the two weeks were up. I wished there was some way I could explain things to Comanche. All he knew was that I wasn't there. But Josie had told me his foot was almost healed, and he would certainly be ready to ride when I got back.

It was my own fault. I got that.

But I was still glad I had helped Stephanie when she needed it. And I'd do it again. But I'd ask Grandpa's permission first. Now I knew he probably would have driven us himself.

Norm and Stephanie's mom had a huge fight on the phone. He yelled at her for leaving Stephanie, and I had to convince Stephanie not to feel guilty about telling Norm that her mom had left.

Hunter texted Stephanie and apologized for leaving her stranded without a ride at the party. He admitted that he was trying to impress the upperclassmen. Stephanie thanked him for the apology.

Star and Clover were both doing fine. We'd called Kirsten that afternoon. Dr. Miller had set Clover's leg, and now she was with Kirsten. They were both drinking eagerly from the bottle, and soon Kirsten would take them to the other rehabilitator. I hoped Kirsten was right about their re-entry to the wild.

The chicken sizzled in the pan and a spicy aroma wove around us.

"I think it's ready," Stephanie said.

"Something smells pretty good in there," Norm called. "We're starving!"

"In a minute!" I yelled. We'd forgotten to warm the taco shells, and I shoved them into the toaster oven.

Stephanie and I started carrying the bowls of ingredients to the dining room, and she arranged them so they looked pretty on the table. The red of the sauce, the green of the lettuce, and the yellow of the cheese looked pretty and appetizing.

I put the toasted taco shells on the table, planning our conversation. I'd come right out and ask Mom and Norm about what happened on their counseling retreat. I'd ask very pointed questions about what was wrong and how they would be fixing things. I'd let them know that it was something they had to do. Because we were a family, and we wanted to stay that way.

"Okay, everything's ready!" I called.

"No, no, wait!" Stephanie cried. She grabbed some matches from a kitchen drawer and, with a trembling hand, lit the candles on the table. The teardrops of light from the two candles wavered, then glowed brighter as they caught. "There!" she said. "Now we're ready."

Stephanie and I went into the family room to call Mom and Norm to the table. Norm was sitting in his La-Z-Boy and Mom was snuggled on the armrest next to him. She was bending down, lightly kissing his forehead.

Stephanie poked me and raised her eyebrows. We went back into the kitchen. Maybe we didn't have to ask all those questions about their retreat after all. Maybe everything was going to be okay.

That night I dreamed that Kirsten released Star and Clover into the wild, their spotted coats flickering in the morning sun. Clover's leg was healed, straight and strong. The little fawns had a quiet grace as they walked beside Kirsten for a few yards. They stopped and gazed at her for a moment, their big ears twitching. When they bounded into the woods, a doe came forward and nosed a greeting, the herd closed protectively around them, and then they disappeared into the dappled sunlit shadows.

Acknowledgements

I'd like to thank my teacher, Ellen Howard, for reading and commenting on this manuscript, and for her wise and sensitive direction. Her support and encouragement have meant so very much to me.

Thank you so much to Sandy Hagen, the wildlife rehabilitator, for allowing me to spend a magical day with her, Clover the fawn, and her other special animals. She was so generous to share her techniques and philosophies with me. And thanks to Clover, for that lick on the arm!

Thanks to Margo Shearon for introducing me to Sandy.

Reverend Jan Brittain of Williamson's Chapel Methodist Church generously allowed me to use the story about the boy in the hospital, which she told during her sermon one Sunday.

My nephew Luke Williams was my quite exuberant subject matter expect for the party and wakeboarding scenes. My brother Pat Williams offered important details as well. Thanks, guys!

And the usual suspects: Chris Woodworth, my dear writing friend, with her incredible sensitivity and instincts; John Bonk, with his unerring sense of a good scene; Ann and Sydney Campanella, with their thoughtful, and gentle comments about character and spirituality; and Deb Waldron, for her practical suggestions and everlasting patience!

Thanks again to Caryn Wiseman, without whom this series would never exist.

Thanks to Kim Childress, my editor, who has been so supportive and insightful. Adding a fifth book to the series was her idea, and I loved getting the chance to write it. I always look forward to the ways in which her comments help me see each scene with new eyes.

I'd also like to thank Candice Frederick, for giving me pep talks when I needed them.

I appreciate all that the staff at Zondervan has done to support this series, from designing such beautiful covers to making bookmarks for me.

My husband Jeff helped me with the veterinary scene. No one is prouder of me than he is, and I thank God for sending him to me.

To my beloved parents and children, thanks for the inspiration for this book.

Sisters in All Seasons Series
by Lisa Williams Kline

Summer of the Wolves

The moving story of two girls and the extraordinary adventure that makes them sisters.

Praise for Summer of the Wolves:

"Kline showcases the difficulties of making blended families work without offering pat answers, and the result is a nicely crafted novel, told from the two girls' perspectives in alternating chapters." *– Booklist*

"Blended families that resist blending are a middle-grade-fiction staple, but this funny, gentle and compassionate story feels fresh, thanks to appealing, closely observed characters, both major and minor, and a compelling setting." *– Kirkus*

Wild Horse Spring

Stepsisters, yes. Friends? Maybe …
Diana and Stephanie are still trying to decide if they like each other when their blended family goes to the Outer Banks of North Carolina for spring break. Soon they're butting heads – again. Diana is crazy about the wild horses, and Stephanie is crazy about the boys – until one guy catches both their interests. But when their crush is accused of committing a crime against the horses, can the stepsisters band together to prove his innocence?

Blue Autumn Cruise

It may take a miracle to save this family vacation.
Full of humor, heartache, friendships, and very real family drama aboard a cruise-ship – where there's no escaping if you want to run away! Join Stephanie and Diana once again as they tread the wavering waters of step-sisterhood.

Winter's Tide

During the bleak and dreary days of winter, Diana continues to be bullied at school, Stephanie continues hiding a painful secret, and both their lives are shaken by two tragic accidents. The girls try pushing through the rockiness in their relationship and facing their challenges, until Stephanie's lie is finally revealed. Can Diana find forgiveness and faith in her darkest hours?

Available in stores and online!

ZONDERVAN®
.com